He knew what she desired. . . .

"I can read minds," Eric whispered. His sharp blue eyes searched hers, as if confirming the secrets he already possessed.

He wasn't joking and Laurie knew it. Cold shivers turning warm, turning hot, coursed down her spine. Her hand froze to the handle of the beer mug. The laughing crowd in the pub seemed to fade away leaving just her and Eric . . . and her thoughts.

"And what," she managed finally, her heart pounding, "exactly what do you read in my mind?"

He hesitated, then refused to answer.

With her nails digging involuntarily into his arm, she prodded, "What do you read?"

"Your thoughts are of me, Laurie. You want to make love with me."

This book is dedicated with love
to Eric Flint,
whose heart is the heart of a Gypsy . . .
like mine

———— ☙ ————

REGAN FOREST
is also the author
of these novels in
Temptation

THE ANSWERING TIDE
STAR-CROSSED
DESERT RAIN
WHEREVER LOVE LEADS
A WANTED MAN
WHEN TOMORROW COMES

Hidden Messages

REGAN FOREST

MILLS & BOON LIMITED
ETON HOUSE, 18-24 PARADISE ROAD
RICHMOND, SURREY TW9 1SR

First published in Great Britain in 1991
by Mills & Boon Limited, Eton House, 18-24 Paradise Road,
Richmond, Surrey TW9 1SR

© Regan Forest 1990

ISBN 0 263 77253 5

21 – 9103

Made and printed in Great Britain

1

THE WIPERS SCULPTED a polished fan from the silky haze of mist on the windscreen as Laurie MacDonald fought her fear of the narrow, unfamiliar road. She shivered and thought of Brian, who had walked away from her at Loch Ness.

The late-afternoon air was taking on the chill of a Highland evening. Dawning Cottage couldn't be much farther, but in this fog it could be difficult to find.

"Great. I'm alone in the middle of nowhere," she said to the swishing windshield wipers, the green hills and the silver-gray air. "An island nobody's heard of, populated by sheep and wind and rain."

The weathered sign of a roadside tavern appeared a short distance away. The Red Wolf. A tavern meant human voices, smiles, the warmth of a meal and directions to Dawning Cottage—all welcome after a long day's drive across the moorlands, the ferry ride, and the narrow, rough roads of the Isle of Lees. The old stone building had the look of a miniature fortress against the elements. Yellow light shone warmly through high windows. Gravel crunched under the wheels of her rented car as Laurie turned into the small parking area.

If the locals were curious about a woman traveling alone, she thought, turning off the engine, so be it. A cold sea wind blew her woolen skirt against her legs as

Laurie walked up the stairway under the sign of a red wolf's head. The wolf's mouth turned in a hideous, canine smile, a vengeful ghost of the creatures that man had exterminated from these Highlands long ago.

She pushed open the heavy door. Lights, smoke, the smells of cooking, and loud, vibrating human voices assaulted her. And in the center of the busy tavern was a spectacle so frightening that Laurie halted, aghast.

A man was hanging upside down. His ankles were clasped by two large men standing on the bar top. A woman was dipping a cloth into a glass filled with whisky, and was squeezing the liquor into his mouth. And there he hung, his heavy, seaman's sweater sliding up, exposing his bare chest.

Horror froze Laurie to the spot; she was unable to move, unwilling to make the slightest motion that would call attention to herself. Had she walked in on a savage, pagan ritual? Her heart thundered with raw fear. Pushed by the wind, the heavy door banged shut behind her, trapping her in this sanctum of madness.

The group was clearly so intent on the ceremony that no one had seen her enter, but Laurie's thoughts of escape were thwarted when the door opened behind her and two men entered, muttering a casual greeting as they pushed on into the room.

The hanging victim, a powerful man, was not fighting for his freedom. He was actually allowing the woman to dribble the whisky into his mouth, even though his arms were free. He pushed aside a fat, gray cat that sauntered up to nuzzle his face, but the cat's tail swung back across his mouth, causing him to flinch and spit.

He sputtered and coughed. With his dark hair curled down over his forehead in a thick tangle and whisky on his chin, he made a flailing gesture and was immediately lowered so his hands could touch the floor. The captors released his ankles and in a second he was standing, pulling down his ivory-white sweater, pushing his hair from his eyes, and wiping his chin with the back of his hand.

A macabre silence lowered over the room, as if someone had flipped a switch and cut all the noise. Every eye was fixed on him with ghoulish curiosity.

Laurie shrank back, trembling, with no idea what was taking place. The abrupt silence was deafening. No one even moved. Laurie could hear only the pounding of her own heart. The object of attention—a rugged, good-looking man—merely stood there, allowing himself to be stared at through the thin fog of cigarette smoke. Aromas of meat, onions and cabbage permeated a room warmed by human bodies. Blending with the fear, the odors were making Laurie queasy.

Unexpectedly a loud hiccup erupted from the man's throat.

Pandemonium broke out. The hiccup seemed a signal for panic as the entire room filled with groans.

Settling onto a bar stool, he poured himself a glass of whisky. "So much for your bloody ideas, Ian Munro."

From the back of the dining area a dark figure skulked past Laurie's still-frozen form. Holding a paper bag in front of him, the bearded man slithered across the room like a cat ready to pounce upon a mouse.

Everyone here is completely insane, the voice screamed inside Laurie's head. *I've stumbled into a madhouse!* When the stalker, unseen, was directly behind the man in the seaman's sweater, he lunged forward with a terrible shriek and pulled the bag over his victim's head.

As the deadly silence fell again, Laurie began to catch on. Her terror turned into laughter deep within her. She fought it desperately.

From inside the bag the low voice growled, "You scared the hell out of me! Get this damn sack off my head!"

"Quick! Take several deep breaths!" a woman said.

To Laurie's surprise, the man did. The paper bag made a crackling sound as he sucked in and out, and the tavern patrons relapsed into silence. This time she held her breath with the rest of them until another, muffled hiccup was heard from inside the paper bag, followed by more crackling and a terrible oath.

A giggle rose into Laurie's throat; she couldn't suppress it. Pagan ceremony, indeed!

"It's no bloody use," the voice within the bag said weakly.

His accent, Laurie noted, was English, not Scottish. The man was quite obviously at his ease among the tavern patrons, but he was not a native of the Isle of Lees.

Another hiccup came as he was removing the paper bag. He took another swallow of whisky and looked dejectedly about the room until his eyes focused on Laurie.

She blinked, feeling foolish because she had stood so long by the door. As he turned into more direct light, a four-inch scar across his jawline became noticeable. The scar was the only flaw, Laurie thought, on one of the most intriguing faces she had ever seen. The ceiling lights brightly reflected the blue of his eyes.

Self-consciously she moved toward a back table and sat down. A middle-aged waiter wearing a red sweater and a broad smile materialized out of the laughter and loud chatter that had resumed.

"A meat pie, perhaps?" the waiter asked. "Or we have a fine roast leg of beef this day."

Amazing, she thought. They were all acting as if nothing in the least extraordinary had just taken place. "I'll have the roast beef and whatever local ale you recommend." She looked past the waiter toward the man at the bar. "Is he all right?"

"Ach, no. I've never in my life witnessed such a case that couldna be cured by Maudie MacFie's upside-down remedy. Cost me three pounds, that bit did. I'll have your order straightaway, miss."

She watched her waiter open an ale behind the bar and set it with a glass on a small tray. When he came around the counter, however, the Englishman intercepted him. Without uttering a word, he rose from the bar stool and took the tray from the waiter's hands.

Blue eyes, bluer still close up, and clear almost to coldness, approached her. He set the tray on her table and proceeded to pour the ale from the bottle into the glass.

"What say you, then? Has American ingenuity come up with an effective means of counteracting hiccups?"

"Am I so obviously American?"

He smiled. "I can recognize an American upside-down—and did."

"Impossible. The waiter must have given you a secret signal after he heard my accent."

The waiter was directly behind him with a plate of food. "Not so, miss! Mind reading is how he does it! True enough, the lad has Gypsy powers."

The hiccup victim sat down across from her, uninvited. When they were alone, he explained, "I told them I could read minds and they believed me."

Laurie studied him, unsure what to make of his exuberant charm, unsure how intoxicated he was. "I thought I'd happened onto a pagan ritual just now. How could you let them suspend you by your ankles?"

"A man can get desperate enough to agree to anything after five or six hours of this." He paused and hiccuped. "How about a contribution here? Every culture has its specialities. There must be a tried-and-true American remedy."

Hungry, she cut a large bite of the hot roast beef and savored its taste. He waited patiently. "Scaring a person usually works."

"I've been scared three times in the past hour. You witnessed the attack with the—*hiccup*—paper bag. I've eaten so much Indian curry my tongue is paralyzed, and I've drunk so much flaming spirits, right side up or upside-down, I'm fairly blitzed."

She asked, "Are you a tourist?"

"From London. I'm doing some temporary work here. That is, I was until this affliction came on me this afternoon. You're—*hiccup*—the last desperate ray of hope."

The scientist in her could have said, Don't be silly. Medical experts confirm that all these hiccup antidotes are old wives' tales. None work, but all work, either way. However, if the afflicted person is too impatient to wait until the problem subsides by itself, shock is the best therapy.

She could have said this, but didn't. Instead, she chose to enter into the spirit of the moment by scratching her head and saying slowly, "According to my great-grandmother, the best cure for hiccups is to place your left foot in a pan of hot water and your right foot in a pan of ice water—simultaneously. The shock of this will do it." She continued to eat her meal calmly.

He looked skeptical. "That must be an American Indian cure."

"No, the Indians relied more heavily on creative methods of fright. I think this came from pioneers of the Texas prairie."

"You're putting me—*hiccup*—on."

She shrugged. "Granted, I've never tried it personally."

"But you recommend it?"

"Highly. Have you tried putting sugar on your tongue?"

"Six cubes, three of them soaked in—*hiccup*—unblended Scotch whisky."

"You have an unusually stubborn case. Maybe the Texas foot cure wouldn't work, either."

He slipped off his shoes. "How much can I lose by trying? I can't take this much longer."

"Oh, dear. It's a cold evening. Maybe you shouldn't." She felt a prickle of unease. "You might catch pneumonia."

"Jamie!" he called, ignoring her warning. "We need two pans of water. . . ." He relayed the requirements to the waiter, who hurried back toward the kitchen, making bets with anyone on the way who was interested.

While she ate, Laurie tried to talk herself out of feeling guilty. There'd have been no guilt if the cure really *had* been her great-grandmother's—or anyone's. She rationalized that hiccup remedies were superstitions; the one she'd made up was as good as any other. If he was silly enough to do this, he deserved wet feet. Anyway, it might work.

Nevertheless, looking at him, Laurie regretted her spontaneity. His smile could not warm the coldness of his eyes. The scar was becoming more noticeable, more sinister.

She said, "If you've had hiccups for several hours, maybe you ought to see a doctor."

"There's no doctor on this side of the island. Are you staying at the Dawning?"

"You're good at lucky guesses."

"Hardly. There's nowhere else to stay. Don't you— *hiccup*—want another drink? My pleasure."

"Thank you, no. I must go. . . it's getting late. Where is Dawning Cottage from here? How far?"

"You're almost there. Carry on down this road another three-quarters of a mile. On your right you'll see a large grove of trees. Turn into—*hiccup*—the trees, and in another hundred meters you'll be at the door."

"Thanks." She finished her drink, anxious to leave before the effects of her foolish suggestion became apparent.

Jamie the waiter was returning, carrying a pan of water.

"Aren't you going to see this through?" he asked. "Your guaranteed pioneer cure?"

"I didn't say it was guaranteed. I suggested you see a doctor."

"If this remedy comes from Texas, I trust it to work. Are you—*hiccup*—from Texas?"

"No."

The pan filled with ice water was placed ceremoniously at his feet. He looked down at it and winced.

"You could get very sick," Laurie protested.

"I once read about a man who had hiccups for forty years. I'd rather be dead. My name's Eric, by the way, in case there's an inquest into my death. Eric Sinclair."

"I'm . . . Laurie MacDonald."

"Aha, MacDonald. Your ancestors walked these very moors when they were populated with more wolves than sheep."

She smiled because it was true. Her initially negative impression of the man had begun to wane, but even so, now that her hunger was alleviated, she couldn't wait to get out of here. She pushed her chair away from the table.

He asked, "Where are you going? You're not staying for this ritual so I can thank you afterwards?"

"The sight of suffering bothers me. Besides, I'd rather not face you if it doesn't work."

"I won't take it personally if it doesn't. Nothing else has worked."

Jamie the waiter brought towels and a second pan of water that sent up a great cloud of steam into the cool air. "Mind not to burn yourself, lad."

Laurie cringed and thought, *I can't believe he's really going to do this.*

With his heavy corduroy slacks rolled to the knee, Eric let out a howl at the shock of the cold water. Immediately he plunged his other foot into the hot. Two waves of water splashed over the rims of the pans and onto the waxed, wooden floor. A low moan of sympathy rolled through the room. He threw his head back and groaned.

Wildly regretting her own mischief, Laurie said, "That's enough! Prolonging the...the treatment is counterproductive."

She stood by with the others, praying it had worked, while he rubbed his feet and legs vigorously with a rough towel. An eager silence settled upon the scene. Two or three people moved in closer to him. Suspense hung heavily on the smoky air.

They waited.

Unsettling blue eyes full of dark secrets met hers. *Some of the locals believe this guy has psychic powers*, she thought. *If those eyes are any indication, maybe he does!* His gaze was something to escape—if one could. Through the tense silence, he didn't even blink.

Had the room not been so quiet, the hiccup wouldn't have resounded so loudly. It convulsed his chest with a jerk. Immediately the moans began again. Eric's broad shoulders sagged.

Laurie rose. "That does it. I'm leaving now."

He looked up at her. "Have you no alternative treatments?"

"Wasn't my last one torment enough? No, I haven't... Well, perhaps yes. A night's sleep. Maybe your hiccups will be gone by morning."

"How can I sleep? I may never sleep again. Every hiccup will wake me."

Slinging the strap of her bag over her shoulder, Laurie smiled with genuine sympathy. "I have faith that you'll triumph over this cursed affliction—eventually."

DESPITE THE LATE HOUR, daylight lingered in the northern skies of summer, over the islands and the sea. The night was silver gray behind the drizzle.

A small sign along the road, leaning as if it had been hit by a vehicle and never straightened, read simply Dawning Cottage. Laurie turned into a long driveway, bordered by dark green lawns and flowers growing in profusion. A flower-lined, stone footpath led up to a peat-covered-roofed, stone house. The two-story cottage could have sprung from the pages of her childhood picture books with its shuttered windows and high, narrow chimneys. A seaside cottage. A setting like those of a hundred novels she had read, a hundred daydreams she had been lost in. Quiet excitement welled up inside her. Somewhere behind the cottage, pounding against the rock foundations of the cliffs, would be the ocean.

Mrs. Jeanne Gunn, clearly responding to the sound of an automobile in the driveway, met her guest at the front door and welcomed her warmly.

"Was I mistaken to expect two people?" she asked politely.

"At the last minute my friend was unable to come."

Laurie followed her hostess up the stairway and into a room on the second floor.

Two single beds took up the space at one end of the room. On the opposite side stood a portable wardrobe, a washstand, and two chairs with a small table between.

"I've closed the shutters to keep out the chill of the wind," Mrs. Gunn said. "But there is a fine view of the sea cliffs. The bath is directly across the hall. I've put flannel sheets on your bed, and you'll find that the small heater works quickly when you need it for dressing. This is one of the coldest summers in years. A fire has nicely warmed the parlor downstairs, and I have tea already made."

Laurie cracked the shutter at the window and looked out through the fog toward the sea she could feel but not see. She closed the shutter again against the cold. "Tea sounds wonderful."

"Breakfast is between eight and nine o'clock, tea every afternoon at four, and supper at eight. Have you had some supper this night?"

"Yes. At the tavern down the road. It's so quiet here, Mrs. Gunn. Do you have other guests?"

"Two others. I've four rooms, and am thankful to have three filled in so cold a summer. Our far shores of Lees are much too remote for most travelers."

"It couldn't be more beautiful."

The woman laughed, obviously delighted, and pulled her woolen shawl tighter across her shoulders.

Shivering, Laurie quickly hung up her few clothes in the wardrobe. Lavender and pale pink wallpaper added little warmth to the atmosphere, but the thick, rose-colored rug and the cushioned seat under the window lent coziness to the pleasant room. She wondered briefly if the craziness of the past two days would continue. The man in the pub and Brian....

You'd have loved this place, Brian, but it's your loss. Some knight you turned out to be. Scared away by Nessie, of all the damn things.

The water of Loch Ness had been a silver glaze yesterday morning. They had stood together in cold, sun-brushed mist, wrapped in a wonderful peace that rose from the moorlands, when the water began to boil and churn in a narrow line before them, and two humps rose darkly, ominously from the mysterious depths—the undulating humps seen by so many people before them. The monster of Loch Ness.

Brian's camera had been at the ready, telescopic lens in place. He'd snapped it at least three times before the humps disappeared, the water trembled, and its wrinkles slowly smoothed.

At first they'd been wild with excitement. Then the implications of what they'd seen had begun to sharpen, and Brian had become short-tempered and utterly unreasonable, carrying on like a maniac about the ridicule they would suffer if they reported the sighting. They had fought over it, and Brian had decided to put an end to everything—his trip and his relationship with her. He had taken the film with him when he left.

Her anger had served to cushion the hurt. At least the remote Isle of Lees was a perfect place to wrestle with her emotions in the wake of Brian's dramatic walkout. She was long past due admitting she had to stop trusting men, once and for all. Men were born to betray women, every last smirking one of them. Why couldn't she ever learn? Brian was the best teacher yet.

All right, I've learned. That's it. I've learned. Keepers of the flame of deceit, beware! Laurie MacDonald has wised up.

The downstairs sitting room was warm and smelled of freshly baked pastries. Mrs. Gunn and a woman wearing a tan woolen blazer over a brown sweater sat sipping tea in front of a peat fire. On the low table was a tray of small cakes and bite-sized pieces of bread topped with cheese or jam. The rug and the drapes had subtle, unmatched floral patterns, and the furniture was heavy and worn. Again, it was so exactly a Scottish farm cottage from her storybooks that the modern clothes seemed out of place.

Jeanne Gunn set down her teacup. "Miss MacDonald, this is Marion Huckles. Marion has come to Dawning to write her memoirs."

The slender woman sat primly with the teacup on her lap, sipping ceremoniously and smiling with caution. She was perhaps fifty. "Memoirs..." Laurie repeated. "How intriguing..."

Mrs. Gunn leaned forward and lowered her voice as if she were afraid of eavesdroppers at the window. "It's all right for me to tell, isn't it, Marion? Marion is writing her memoirs under the assumed name of Margo Mayberry DuBois."

"It is my collection of rather outrageous love stories," Marion Huckles volunteered, peering over the dark rim of her glasses. "Based, of course, on my own life's experiences."

Laurie tried not to stare. If anyone she'd ever met gave the appearance of a dismal, unimpassioned spinster, this woman did. "A whole . . . uh . . . collection?"

"Quite so."

"Fascinating." Laurie helped herself to tea and a vanilla biscuit and couldn't resist adding, "The DuBois collection. Sounds very French, too, and outrageously . . . boudoirish?"

This brought a smile from the author and a laugh from Mrs. Gunn.

"I've never quite understood what is behind the desire to write one's intimate memories," Jeanne Gunn said gently, still in a secretive kind of whisper. "Is it to relive the past or is it perhaps to . . . to shock? Will your memoirs shock, Marion?"

Miss Huckles DuBois's pale eyes suddenly came more alive. "Perhaps, Mrs. Gunn, should this collection be published, it will shock. This I cannot help. I believe it is cleansing to the soul to bare all. Don't you agree, Laurie?"

"Uh . . . well . . . I suppose that depends on the memories. There are the comedies and there are the tragedies. . . ."

"Oh, yes. One must attempt an overall balance for the sake of one's audience. Alternate the tragic with the light."

Laurie had only the vaguest idea where this conversation was going, but the subject of love affairs was definitely her least favorite at the moment. "More power to you, I say, Marion. I sure couldn't do it. My memoirs would read like *The Perils of Pauline*."

Mrs. Gunn sat back contentedly. "Laurie, what brings you to the Isle of—?" She was interrupted by a wildly honking car horn from the driveway, followed by loud voices.

Alarmed, she was on her feet at once. "Oh, saints! What on earth?"

She rushed toward the door, with Laurie a pace behind. Marion set down her teacup with controlled precision and said calmly, "It's either Eric Sinclair, or else MacBean's pigs are loose in the flower beds again."

"Pigs don't yell and beep," Jeanne Gunn responded, pushing the door open against the night wind. "Something's happened!"

In the gray, damp twilight, three men lifted another from the back seat of a car. Pulling her dark red shawl tightly around her shoulders, Mrs. Gunn rushed out, shouting questions.

Laurie stopped on the front step and watched the men haul the limp figure to the house. Eric? It had to be! The man being carried was wearing a thick, light-colored sweater and only one shoe.

Excited, muffled words tangled with the sound of the wind rustling the tree branches overhead.

She thought with horror, *They went too far with their damned remedies*...and muttered aloud, "Lord in heaven, they've killed him!"

2

MARION HUCKLES pushed in front of Laurie, holding a lace-trimmed handkerchief over her mouth. "Someone has been killed?"

Mrs. Gunn rushed down the steps. "It's Mr. Sinclair! What happened to him?"

"Accident," one of his bearers answered, grunting under the weight.

"He's out cold," said another.

"And bleeding." They reached the porch.

"Saints be!" Jeanne Gunn wailed as she spun around and called back over her shoulder, "Take him to the sitting room!"

By the time the men carried in the unconscious man, she had secured a blanket and thrown it over the sofa. While the men lowered their burden, she grabbed a tea towel from the serving table to place under his bleeding head.

Eric moaned and twitched, but did not open his eyes. One of the men leaned close to him. "Bad fall he took."

"How did he fall?" Mrs. Gunn asked, examining the wound beneath the blood that shone in his dark hair.

One of the burly Scots cocked his head toward Laurie helplessly, almost apologetically. "Eric was putting on his shoes, teetering back in the chair, when Robbie MacDuff crept up behind him unbeknownst and popped off a racing gun. Loud as a cracker it was. Eric jumped like a scared rabbit, and his chair slipped in the spilled water on the floor. His head hit the table leg."

Oh no, not the water. . . . Laurie weakly cursed herself.

"Knocked himself out dead," he added.

"Don't say the word dead," Marion muttered, leaning close to the unconscious Eric. "He certainly isn't dead."

Mrs. Gunn was blotting the blood. "What childish nonsense! This cut isn't serious, but the blow must have been fierce. There's danger of concussion. Or did he pass out from too much ale? Surely. I can smell it on him. . . ." She bent her head to his broad chest to listen to his heart.

"Should we be packing him off to a doctor, Jeanne?"

"It's a dreadful long and rough distance." She shook him gently. "Eric! Come on, open up those bonny blue eyes!"

He stirred, muttering something incomprehensible. His eyes fluttered open.

"Who am I?" Jeanne Gunn asked him.

"Don't you know?" His voice was a husky whisper.

"What is my name?"

"I haven't got amnesia, Mrs. Gunn. I've got a devil of a headache." He touched the wound on his head and groaned. "What'd I hit?"

"The table leg," one of his companions answered.

Mrs. Gunn straightened. Hands on her hips, she scowled. "Putting on shoes, did you say? And why would his shoes be off, if I dare ask?"

"You don't want to know...." Eric mumbled, eyes closing.

"Hmph. I'm sure that's so. This bump is the size of an apple. Head wounds bleed profusely, but the bleeding is lighter now. I predict that with some rest and a bit of looking after, you'll survive."

"Unless there's a concussion," Marion reminded them primly. She glared disapprovingly at the three men, who had cleaned every crumb of bread and pastry from the tea tray.

Unconcerned by the assault on her food, the landlady was inspecting the wound once again. "We'll have to watch you for signs of concussion. So don't carry on when I wake you in the night to see if you're conscious. I expect you to behave."

The wounded man moved his head with effort. He looked around the warm, dimly lighted room until his eyes came to rest on the dark-haired young woman in a pale pink sweater who stood between the sofa and the fireplace, watching him in silence.

"Laurie MacDonald," he said. "In a roundabout way, the Texas cure seems to have worked...."

Firelight glowed on his handsome face as she gazed down at him. His eyelids were drooping so heavily, he appeared to be fighting to stay conscious.

"I'm so sorry you were hurt," she said gently.

"I'm not ... hurt."

"Really?" Marion was brushing pastry crumbs from the linen tablecloth. "What are you, if not hurt?"

"Dazed. Slightly, temporarily dazed."

Mrs. Gunn said, "You very definitely classify as injured, Eric lad, possibly seriously. Which means you'll remain here tonight, where it's warm and I can keep an eye on you." She rose to bid his three bearers good-night.

"I'm going upstairs to my room," Eric protested, his eyes closed.

"And how will you manage to climb the steps?" Marion challenged, shivering in cold air let in by the open door.

He lay very still. "Miss Huckles, you're always ped-dling doom...."

"For an unconscious lad you do a lot of talking," Jeanne Gunn said as she returned with a small pan of water and two towels, one of which she placed under his head, ignoring his moans of pain. "Now. Let's see about cleaning and disinfecting the cut."

"I'm going upstairs," he repeated, as if delirious. "I can't sleep here. My head hurts like bloody hell. Don't touch it."

Laurie asked, "How can I help?" Offering assistance was the least she could do.

"Pull off his shoe, if you will. I wonder where the other one is." Jeanne ignored another loud groan as she dabbed at the wound. "Marion, dear, in the cupboard in the upstairs hall are sheets and blankets. Would you be so kind as to bring some down? Steady there, Eric, my lad, don't twitch so. Saints be, what a bump this is!"

His eyes were still tightly closed. "I don't feel well...."

"I should think not! You were knocked completely out."

Laurie was caught in a tangle of guilt and disbelief. The man would not be lying here barely conscious, with a possible concussion, if she hadn't made up that

stupid water remedy. Still, it wasn't her fault some idiot sneaked up behind him and startled him off balance. And what kind of man would go to such extremes
to cure a case of hiccups that would eventually go away,
if he was patient? An obsessive personality, obviously.

Firelight flickering on the walls, on his sweater and
his pale face, lent eeriness to an already less than real
scene. It was another in the series that had unfolded
since her arrival in Scotland and the second in one
night. Marion returned with blankets, set them on the
back of the sofa and stood watching Mrs. Gunn ad-
minister first aid. Her pale eyes shone with interest,
though her face remained passive.

The patient jerked and let out a wail. Mrs. Gunn
drew her hand away slowly. "Disinfectant. It stings a
wee bit. Now I'll just apply a bandage...."

He protested, "You're not going to put tape in my
hair?"

"A doctor would shave at least half your head,"
Marion declared.

His face was ashen. In spite of his complaining, he
made no attempt to move. Being knocked unconscious had clearly left him groggy and in pain. And it
had left him without the strength to protest as the three
women made up the sofa under and around his heavy
body, jostling him about. As soon as this unpleasant
task was completed, he rolled onto his good side, faced
the fire and sighed pathetically.

Across the room they chatted in hushed tones while
they sipped a fresh pot of tea. Every now and then a low
moan would reach them.

Jeanne Gunn had donned a white apron when she went to the kitchen for the water. She tugged at the apron pockets and leaned closer to her two companions. "When concussion is suspected, the person must be wakened every hour during the night. Our plan, therefore, is to divide into shifts."

"In that case, I volunteer for first shift," Marion offered, glancing at her tiny wristwatch. "I simply cannot wake before seven in the morning, and I must get proper sleep in order to function and stay regular."

"I, on the other hand," Jeanne Gunn said, "am accustomed to getting up at four o'clock every morning."

"Which leaves me with the middle shift," Laurie concluded. The deepest hours, she thought, when there was the most danger of his not waking.

When the others went upstairs, Marion settled into the chair under a lamp with a thick book.

Laurie's room was cold. At ten-thirty, light was still showing through the curtains—a bleak light too bright for the moon, too dim for the sun. Twilight. She shivered in bed until her body heat warmed it, and for half an hour she lay awake, unable to quiet her restless thoughts.

Brian's face swam before her. How strange his abrupt exit from her life had been. He'd been so angry over her eagerness to report their sighting of the monster—so afraid of their being laughed at. But no one laughed at Nessie. The more she thought about it, the less his leaving in a fit of anger made sense. And his eyes— they'd been less angry than sad and pleading when he'd said his last goodbye.

Men.

Brian had wanted to come to Britain with her. Insisted. Added his plans to her trip. They would tour some of Scotland, then go to Lees together. He had planned to stay three days with her on Lees, the last three days of his vacation time, and she would remain to research the Celtic ceremonial site.

In the year she had known him, his unpredictable behavior had surfaced from time to time, but he had never gone berserk before. Maybe he just couldn't deal with the implications of seeing something he didn't believe existed. But it was more than that—Brian had acted damned weird. Some undefined thing about him had kept a wall between them, always—a wall like Plexiglas—impossible to see, impossible to penetrate.

Why hadn't he just let her come alone, instead of wanting to be a part of it and then retreating? He'd said he didn't want to hurt her. Why had he, then?

Men. Players of games.

The eyes that Laurie pictured as she drifted toward sleep weren't Brian's. They were those of an Englishman, eyes so full of mischief that they had alarmed her when he sat down across from her at the table in the tavern. Blue eyes, capable of reading the thoughts of strangers.

Blue eyes distracting her anger, distracting her hurt. Brian had been great fun, but she had never been able to truly love him through the invisible barrier. Freedom wasn't so bad; there was a certain peace....

THE SHAKING STARTLED HER. In the dim light from the hallway Marion's pale, powdered face looked ghostly.

"It's one o'clock," she said. "Your turn to try to sleep in that dreadful chair and to wake the growling giant every hour."

The cold of the room assaulted Laurie as she sat up. "How is he?"

Marion hugged her notebook against her breast, as if she were afraid it would leap away from her, given the slightest chance.

"He moans," Marion said. "I can't bear the sound of a man moaning. That is, I can't bear a *sleeping* man's moans. A man awake...that's another matter entirely."

Laurie yawned. "You shock me, Marion."

"Indeed? I didn't think one could shock an American."

The remark wasn't worth responding to at one-thirty in the morning. Noting that Marion was wearing a woolen blanket as a shawl, Laurie pulled the top bed blanket up over her shoulders and slipped into her shoes. "Is the fire still burning downstairs?"

"Oh yes. The room is quite comfortable."

"Thank God. It's freezing up here. Okay, I'm on my way." Yawning, hating the dull ache of fighting off the grip of needed sleep, she followed the blanketed Marion into the hallway. "Does Eric Sinclair appreciate this, Marion?"

"I doubt it. He threatened me with bodily harm each time I shook him awake. The worst was sitting there, worrying what to do if he didn't wake up. Phone a doctor in the village, I suppose."

"What village do you mean?"

"Fyfe's Landing. It's the only one."

"The grumbling may be a good sign. The man is probably too ornery to actually crack his skull."

"He's a rogue," Marion said with disdain as she opened the door of her room. "Englishmen who are rogues are the worst kind. Believe me, I know."

Laurie shook her head, smiling. Marion Huckles DuBois was a study in contradiction—a woman with the demeanor and appearance of one's drab maiden aunt who claimed to be a seasoned seductress. Or was she genuine? Marion was a fascinating mystery she would have to explore.

The blanket dragged behind her like a bridal train, Laurie thought ironically as she made her way down the dimly lighted stairs. The combination of her flannel nightgown and walking shoes was not, however, bridelike, and she resented Eric Sinclair for putting her through this ordeal.

The tavern patrons had been acting absolutely ridiculously. How far would they have gone with their silly hiccup cures if Eric had remained conscious? Of course, if she hadn't suggested the damn water torture, the floor wouldn't have been wet and slick.

The parlor was equally dim; light came only from the glow of the peat fire and the reading lamp in one corner, above an overstuffed chair. Laurie had neglected to ask whether Marion had roused him just before coming upstairs. If she hadn't—wanting to avoid getting barked at—then it was up to Laurie to do it.

She stood over him for a full minute, watching him sleep. Marion's epithet played like a note from a nagging tune: rogue. He had the handsome face of a genuine rogue, all right, a face no woman could ever tire

of. The scar—the mark of a savory or sinister past—
was barely visible in the shadows. Eric lay on his back,
the only position in which he could fit on the couch.
One arm was above his head, the other across his
stomach. His head was turned toward the fire, his lips
were almost closed. There was blood on his sweater.

In the firelight he looked more dead than alive. A
rumble of fear coursed through her. A man would have
to be hit hard to be knocked unconscious. Or would it
depend on how much he'd had to drink?

She knelt beside him and touched his shoulder. "Eric?
Eric, are you all right? Wake up."

He moaned and stirred a little.

"Come on! Open your eyes."

With another sound of protest, his eyelids fluttered.
She shook him gently and said his name again.

With an effort he opened his eyes. Pain discouraged
him from moving his head.

So fierce was his stare that Laurie involuntarily
straightened, wondering what it was that had so captured his eye.

His voice came from far away. "Is that you, Laurie
MacDonald?" What a picture she made wearing a halo
of firelight in tousled hair, wide lace at the neck of her
pink nightgown.

She tried to smile. "Good, you're cognizant."

"For a moment I thought I was in the chamber of
angels...."

"Oh, please. Only a guy in pretty sad shape would
come up with that cliché."

"What cliché?"

"The old, wake-up-thinking-she's-an-angel cliché. Chamber of angels . . . Give me a break."

"It's not a cliché. It's a brothel in London."

Laurie drew in her breath, angered. "Maybe I should let you die!"

He smiled, then his eyelids closed weakly.

He looked pale enough and feeble enough, lying there, for her to regret her outburst. She said, "You're not going to die."

"I know. Why are you here in the witching hour?"

"Humanitarian reasons."

"Is it humanitarian to keep waking me, when I'm trying like the devil to sleep?"

"In an inverted sort of way. If you don't wake, it means you have managed to get yourself a concussion, in which case it's to a hospital, if there is one in this wilderness. Waking you is the kindest thing I've ever done. Does your head hurt?"

"Yes."

"Can I get you anything? Water?"

"Please don't say . . . that word."

"Water?"

He touched his abdomen. "I have to get up. I can't move, but I have to get up. All that beer I drank has gone through me."

"Great. All right, I'll help you."

He stared up at her.

"I mean, you can lean on me. Can you walk?"

"What choice have I got?" He moved the blanket aside, complaining as he sat up, holding his head. "At least the cursed hiccups are gone. . . ."

With Laurie gently pulling on his arms, he got to his feet.

"You're wobbling horribly," she said.

"If I start to fall, protect yourself. I didn't realize how small you are."

"If you start to fall, it's your head we'd better be worried about."

His body, leaning against her, felt heavier with every step. They weaved precariously through the unheated hallway to the bathroom door.

"Be careful," she warned. "Don't lock the door."

"Your nanny role isn't convincing. This isn't going to be easy, Laurie."

"If I hear a deafening crash, I'll come in after you. Otherwise the challenge is yours."

She paced, waiting for him, shivering because she had shed the blanket, and half expecting to hear the deafening crash. The man was so groggy that he could barely stand up.

Nevertheless, he was soon safely back on the couch again, sitting with his head in his hands and asking, "Would you have any aspirin?"

"Yes, in my bag upstairs. I'll get them."

He was still in the same position when she returned with the aspirin and a pitcher of water. She held two tablets out for him.

"Two won't do it," he said as soon as he had swallowed them. He reached for the bottle she had set down on the table.

"Don't get carried away."

"Me? I never get carried away."

"I noticed that the first time I saw you—hanging upside down."

He looked up and fixed his eyes on her so intensely that she drew back, conscious once again of her disheveled appearance. Huskily he said, "You're beautiful, Laurie MacDonald."

"I know how great I look right now," she countered, refusing to be so affected by him. "You look pretty good yourself. In fact, you've turned the color of a corpse since you got up. Are you all right?"

"I feel terrible."

She drew closer. "You're not going to throw up, are you?"

"I did that in the WC."

"Oh, no! Nausea is one of the symptoms of concussion!"

"It's also a symptom of uncontrolled consumption of Scottish spirits. Don't look so concerned, Laurie. Your worry is for nothing. This is a middling—if undignified—condition. I've been bashed about a lot worse than this in my day."

"You? An English gentleman?"

"I wasn't born an English gentleman."

He lay back on the couch. "Why are we keeping each other up all night?"

"You look very sleepy."

"Misleading. I'm a borderline insomniac. I could sleep while Miss Huckles was sitting over there like an ice sculpture. But you in your nightgown . . . can make me forget I am an English gentleman, which actually I'm not. . . ." His voice was becoming sleepy as the pain relievers began to take effect.

It would be easy now, she thought, to talk him back into needed sleep. She balanced on the arm of the sofa near his feet. "You weren't born an English gentleman? Who could guess? Where were you born?"

His eyes were closed. "I have no idea. I was stolen from the Gypsies."

Laurie's eyebrows shot up. "You were what?"

"Stolen...at a very early age...." Laurie watched her dark Gypsy drift back toward slumber. How many surprises, she mused, could one vacation hold?

3

JEANNE GUNN APPEARED out of the early-morning silence, dressed in black slacks and two gray sweaters.
The fire had burned down and dim yellow-gray sunlight was glowing through the window.

"You aren't asleep, Laurie?" she whispered.

"I haven't slept much. What time is it?"

"Four o'clock. How's the laddie?"

Laurie sat up stiffly and stretched. "He gets more
grumpy by the hour. I think he's all right, Mrs. Gunn.
His head is too hard to crack on a table leg."

"Aye. That's so." She glanced at Eric. He was making sensual sounds as he slept. "He's soundly asleep and
dreaming dreams we would not want to know. Is the
swelling down?"

"I didn't feel the bump."

Gathering teacups onto the tray, Mrs. Gunn whispered, "I'll be working in the kitchen. I'll come in and
check on him from time to time until he realizes he's still
among the living."

Wrapped in the blanket, Laurie trudged up the stairs.
Four in the morning, she thought wearily, and it was
already light outside.

In her room, standing by the window, she heard a
distant roaring. The ocean? Cool, dewy air, fresh with
a salty tang, touched her face when she opened the

window, but the echoing noise she heard could not be the ocean, because there was no rhythm. It sounded more like a waterfall.

She must be mistaken. Laurie closed the window and rolled into bed, hoping for three or four hours of sleep. Sleep had been impossible in the chair across the room from the enigmatic Englishman.

Mystery surrounded Eric Sinclair. He'd mentioned he was working here on the Isle of Lees. Doing what, she couldn't imagine. There was nothing here except the wild moorlands and the sea wind. And this charming guest house and the peace.

Brian would have liked the peace. He would have taken five hundred pictures of the quaint surroundings and followed up with a dozen hours of organizing and labeling each slide. Laurie herself had been subjected to his slide shows of the Virgin Islands and Baja California in the early days of their friendship, when she'd still felt the need to apologize for falling asleep during the torturous, armchair trips. Brian's photographs had never included people. On this trip he had taken two dozen photos at Loch Ness, none of her, but at least three of Nessie.

Brian liked peace, but he hadn't left her with any. Men were undecipherable. Hotheaded Americans, stray, wisecracking Englishmen—all unreadable. Water monsters were less elusive, less mystifying. More predictable . . . probably more deserving of a woman's love. . . .

SHE SLEPT until eight o'clock. There were no sounds or signs of activity in the upstairs hallway when she crossed to the bathroom in her flannel nightgown. Her robe had been too bulky to fit into her suitcase; now she wished she'd bought and packed a light one.

In the breakfast room, an alcove off the main dining room, Marion was at breakfast, sipping tea. Sunlight was shining through the east window onto the white linen tablecloth, making the silver sparkle. Dressed in a dark skirt and sweater with a white collar and cuffs, Marion was reading a romance novel. The dark circles under her eyes were testimony to a night of missing sleep.

"How is the patient this morning?" Laurie asked, sitting down across from her.

Marion glanced up from her book. "He's disappeared."

"What?"

Mrs. Gunn pushed through the swinging door from the kitchen, carrying a plate of bacon, eggs and toast, which she set in front of Marion. "Mr. Sinclair has not disappeared," she corrected. "Except from the parlor. He told me he needed a wee bit of fresh air. The last I saw of him, he was wobbling down the glen."

"He ought to have sense enough to rest," Marion said, setting aside the novel and adjusting the napkin on her lap. She was looking down at her plate, absorbed in appraisal, as if she were an art critic examining a picture.

"He is by his nature a restless man," Jeanne Gunn said. "There is tea and coffee and juice on the sideboard, Laurie. Help yourself. I'll bring your breakfast straightaway."

Marion ate so primly that she dabbed her lips with her napkin after each bite. While Laurie poured herself coffee at the sideboard, Marion asked, "Do you find Eric attractive?"

Laurie turned. "I imagine everyone would. Don't you?"

"Perhaps, in a rough-edged sort of way. That scar on his jaw, for instance. I mentioned once that it might be a knife scar, and he said it was from a fight. But in actual fact I don't believe it for a moment. He finds some twisted delight in deliberately teasing me."

Sitting down again with coffee and a glass of freshly squeezed orange juice, Laurie said, "It could be true. He seems the type who wouldn't shrink from a fight. I met him in the tavern last night. Things were friendly in there, but unruly. The Englishman fits perfectly into that atmosphere of rowdiness."

"Fits in? He instigates it, I'm sure. That ridiculous accident last night was plainly the result of loathsomely childish behavior. Obviously the man fell because he was wellied to his eyeballs."

Laurie smiled. "He wasn't that . . . uh . . . wellied, Marion. We talked a little. He told me he was working in this area. What work does he do?"

"He says he's here to record sounds of the sea and the wilderness with all that electronic equipment he drags about. According to Eric the demand for tapes of nature sounds is a booming business. But I think all he's captured so far is the sound of rain. He's been here four days and it's rained every day. Now today we have a lovely, clear morning and he's probably too feeble to carry the equipment outside." Marion sighed. "Hanging about a tawdry tavern . . . dreadful."

Their hostess swung into the room again, set a plate in front of Laurie and went to the sideboard to pour herself a cup of tea.

"I'll say one thing for him," Jeanne Gunn observed. "I've never seen an Englishman so rapidly accepted by the locals."

Marion sniffed. "Ruffians band together naturally. Mud blends with mud."

"Why do you dislike him so?" Laurie asked, knowing she wouldn't get an honest answer. Eric Sinclair was an attractive man by any woman's standards, and Marion Huckles DuBois fancied herself a temptress. He was, of course, much younger than her, but Laurie suspected Marion's problem was one of injured pride. Perhaps the handsome scoundrel had not responded to her irresistible charms as she felt he should.

"I hardly dislike him," Marion answered. "I merely consider him an underbred clod."

Laurie cut a generous piece of sausage. "I find him a little brittle, but not a clod. Not the least clodlike, do you think, Mrs. Gunn?"

Jeanne laughed and stirred more sugar into her tea. "Once, long ago, this little island was a haven for pirates. My comely guest, whose surname is Scottish, not English, by the way, makes me remember the pirate stories. His scar, combined with that . . . untamed expression in the eyes. He can be a wee bit frightening. But I like him. Everyone does, except our Lady Marion."

"It's his charm," Marion said with sour sarcasm, as if she were the only one who wasn't taken in.

Laurie looked out through the lace curtains, picturing pirate ships lying off this remote coast and villainous, scarred and scruffy seamen stalking along the shore. Jeanne looked at Eric's untamed eyes and thought of pirates. Marion, if she was to be believed, saw a renegade and misfit. Laurie also saw the wildness, the mystery of Eric's eyes, but he was neither pirate nor misfit. His were the eyes of a Gypsy. Gypsies had once claimed the glens and hills of this island, too.

To distract herself Laurie spoke. "What a lovely clear morning. Last night I heard a sound like a waterfall."

"It is a waterfall," Jeanne answered. "The river falls into the gorge just before it reaches the sea. Hiking can be a wee bit treacherous hereabouts. The rocks are slick where the river tumbles down the mountain, and the cliffs are quite steep. Have you good hiking boots?"

Laurie was by now well into her breakfast of fried eggs, bacon and sausage, and toasted homemade bread. "Not boots, but I have some pretty sturdy shoes," she answered, chewing.

Marion dabbed her lips with the napkin. "Jeanne tells me you're staying here for two or three weeks. Might you be a writer also?"

"No, an anthropologist. I chose this island because of the archaeological evidence of ancient Druids. The Druids are a special interest of mine."

Mrs. Gunn's eyes brightened. "You'd mean the sacrificial altar in the hills past Lochenmore!"

"Yes. I want to have a look at it. But I also came to enjoy the scenery, relax, read, and catch up on some reports." *And get my life together*, she thought. She finished a slice of toast. "I write research reports. Hardly the fascinating sort of material that Marion is working on."

Jeanne rose, took the teapot from the sideboard and refilled Marion's cup. "Will you have more, Laurie?"

"No, thanks. I can't wait to get outside. I spent months reading about the beauty of Lees, and now that I'm here, I want to experience it." She pushed away from the table.

"I hope you brought your waterproof gear," Marion said. "It rains here almost every day with no warning whatsoever."

"I came well equipped," Laurie answered. Equipped for the rain, at least, she told herself. Unexpected rainfall was a surprise only if one trusted the skies.

The skies of Lees were moody and constantly shifting—like the eyes of Eric Sinclair.

LOW STONE WALLS snaked across the landscape. Sheep grazed peacefully—puffs of white against the green hillsides. A few hundred feet from the back of Dawning Cottage, the craggy terrain dropped so abruptly into a steep valley that in darkness a stranger walking there could easily fall to his or her death.

From a ledge that overlooked the rock walls, Laurie discovered the narrow, tumbling waterfall. At the bottom, pastel rainbows formed in its misty spray. She stood for a moment, breathing in the fragrance of green earth and water.

Two full minutes passed before she turned and saw him.

Eric sat against a tree, knees up, his head leaning into his arms. He was wearing earphones. Beside him was a portable cassette player. So concentrated was he on whatever he was listening to, he hadn't seen her approach through the trees. He didn't move, not a muscle. The breeze caressed his hair softly around the taped bandage. He was wearing the same clothes he had slept in, the same sweater, spattered with his blood. She watched him for several more moments before she went her own way, down a steep and narrow pathway toward the rainbows.

Wildflowers bloomed in profusion. Bracken lined the valley walls. Halfway down, she caught a glimpse of silver through the trees. The Atlantic Ocean. Climbing down was not difficult; the drop was not as steep as it had first appeared, but the gorge became very narrow as she descended. By the time she reached the bottom, only a tiny, gurgling stream was left to dance and tumble to the rocky shore.

The sea opened up before her, crashing in over great rocks. At high tide it would not be possible to walk all the way to the bottom.

It was cold on the rocky beach, and Laurie was shivering by the time she started back. The climb warmed her body.

At the top again, a little out of breath, she found Eric in the same spot under the tree, but now he was stretched out on his stomach in the grass, arms above his head, and still wearing the headphones.

His eyes were closed; he didn't see her walk toward him and sit down on the grass beside him. But before long, maybe feeling a presence near, he opened his eyes.

She smiled.

He slid off the earphones carefully to avoid touching the painful lump.

"How's your head?" she asked.

"I wish my head belonged to somebody else."

"How can you listen to music while you have a headache?"

"Music soothes me. It's about the only thing that can."

"I'm sure it has to be the right kind of music."

He stared at her for a moment before he sat up, pushing his dark hair from his eyes. "What kind of music do you like?"

"Oh...many kinds. Eric, you don't look very good."

Rubbing the stubble on his chin, he pulled an unhappy face. "Maybe I should have gone upstairs to bed after the Gestapo woke me at five this morning. Mrs. Gunn decided to apply ice to my lump. Who could sleep after that? I came out here to escape. What type of music do you prefer most?"

"Classical, I suppose."

Eric was thoughtful. "Mmm. Me, too. Good omen. Why did you decide to come to Lees, Laurie? Looking for isolation?"

"Looking for remnants of Druid sacrifice."

"Ah. The standing stones. How long will you stay?"

"Two weeks, possibly three."

As he looked at her with new intensity, the color of his eyes changed.

He said, "I want to apologize for the imbecile remark I made last night. It was inexcusable, even though I was probably delirious at the time."

"Of course you were. You took one look at me and thought you were in a brothel. Very flattering."

"I was in a semicomatose condition. Besides, I was just wising off."

"Wising off in a delirious, semicomatose condition?"

"You were wearing a nightgown with lace, and the firelight was shining in your hair." He looked down at the grass pensively. "There is no brothel by that name."

"I don't believe you."

"Your words wound. What would I know about brothels? I wanted to get in the last word. I'm bad that way."

"I know."

Eric rubbed his forehead despondently. "You were patient and I was pathetic and I'm still pathetic. I apologize for my bedraggled appearance. And forgive me for asking this, but why is a woman as lovely as you on holiday alone?"

"That's a shockingly macho remark, Eric. But to satisfy your rugged curiosity, I didn't start out alone. My friend and I parted company at Loch Ness after we saw the monster."

He jerked to attention. "You saw Nessie?"

She looked at his eyes. "Oh, if I don't tell someone, I'll burst! Yes, we saw it. We were on the western shore, looking out at the water early in the morning. The lake was perfectly still, smooth as glass. And suddenly the water began to boil and churn for a line of several yards, and two black bumps appeared on the surface. It was just like the pictures! Can you believe we actually saw it? People look for years, and our very first morning there . . . we saw it!"

"I'll be damned."

"You don't believe me. You think I'm crazy!"

"I believe you."

"No. You don't. You'd be laughing right now if it wouldn't hurt your head to laugh."

Eric didn't smile. "I wouldn't laugh. I've seen Nessie myself, some years ago. Your sighting must have caused a great stir."

Laurie sighed and picked a blue wildflower. Gazing at the flower, she answered, "No, it caused no stir at all. We didn't tell anyone."

"Why not? How could you help it? Others might—"

"I wanted to," she interrupted, feeling the anger again. "But he didn't. Brian said we'd be laughed at and there would be a great fuss with the press, and he was in no mood for it. He even got photos of the monster through a telescopic lens. We argued about it, and he got so angry he just . . . decided to leave. I took him to the nearest train station and he said goodbye forever, and I don't know why the hell I'm telling you all this. I still can't believe any of it."

Eric fell into a strange silence.

I was mad to tell him, she thought.

He looked out through the trees at the shine of falling water over the rocks. The waterfall was brilliant in the sun. At length he asked softly, "Brian was your lover?"

She sighed shakily, twirling the flower between her thumb and forefinger. "Yes. And my friend. We always got along so well before . . . before that cursed monster."

His gaze moved slowly from the waterfall to her eyes. "Brian never told you he was married?"

The question jabbed like the blade of a sword. Laurie tried to stare him down. "What are you talking about? Why would you say a thing like that?"

"Maybe I shouldn't have."

"Why did you?"

"Brian is married, Laurie. I'd wager my left ear that he's married."

She shook her head. "No! I've known him for a year. . . ."

"Then he lied for a year." Eric looked away. "I've heard Americans are notorious for lying about their marital status. Your ex-Brian is a scoundrel."

"Eric, that blow on the head knocked you senseless. How . . . dare you . . . ?" She tossed the flower aside. "How dare you comment on matters you know absolutely nothing about?"

"Sorry," he said, rubbing the stubble on his chin. He didn't sound sorry at all.

An uncomfortable silence ensued. Laurie's brain was racing.

Finally she asked hesitantly. "Why do you think so?"

"Pure logic. What scared him away was the threat of all the publicity. Photographs of the two of you. A Nessie sighting might have made world news."

"Well . . . he . . ."

"Think back over everything, Laurie. I have a feeling that if you put everything together, you'll realize you've been deceived."

She fell into silence, thinking back, as he suggested. Remembering unexplained absences, strange emergencies, reasons why his "roommate" was always utilizing the apartment she never saw. And he took no photos of her, not ever.

She dropped her head. "Oh . . . damn. . . ."

"Did you love him?" Eric asked.

"In a way...yes. I thought..." She turned to him, her chin lifted defensively. "What kind of mind do you have that you could analyze people that way? It's absolutely eerie!"

"It isn't eerie. I'm just observing."

"It's more than that, Eric. It's . . . What the hell is it? Some kind of . . . of Gypsy wizardry? Or were you delirious when you told me last night you were stolen from the Gypsies? Who steals children from Gypsies, I'd like to know?" Even this, she thought desperately, was better than continuing the discourse on Brian.

"It's a complex story," Eric answered.

"I'm sure it is."

"But true."

"Sure."

"My mother was supposed to be a Gypsy. My father, who was not, stole me from the Gypsy camp one night, because he didn't want his son to be a Gypsy waif. My father was a professional, traveling gambler. He was never sure whether he married my mother or not, because he never knew if the Gypsy ceremony was legal." He glanced at her. "My father has always stuck stubbornly to this story, so it might be true. On the other hand, knowing him, it might be a lie. I rarely see him anymore. We fell out and I don't—" His voice cut off, but not before Laurie detected that what he was cutting off was hurt . . . some deep and hidden hurt. It brought her to attention.

He covered it, continuing, "I don't remember my mother, only my father's mistresses. But once I had a dream about a woman with long, dark hair and scarlet clothes trimmed with silver, who whispered my name over and over."

Laurie felt very shaky. Her mind kept sliding back to Brian, her hurt erupting into fury. It all added up. Brian *had* lied to her. She ached for the chance to confront him and deeply resented the fact that Eric had figured out what she hadn't.

Nevertheless, Eric's improbable biographical sketch had the power to distract even these thoughts. "You're making up the whole story," she accused.

"Who would want to make up a life like that?"

"Someone who wants sympathy, maybe."

"What do I need sympathy for? You're the one who's just lost a lover."

She watched him carefully—watched his lips move as he spoke. "Who are you really, Eric? You describe a child who could have been the toughest kid on the block, yet you admittedly prefer classical music and you talk like an educated man."

"I am an educated man. Two years at Cambridge. But I didn't complete my studies. It was too bitter a struggle to work my way through, added to the fact that I had to give up too much fresh air. My father had more to teach me about mastering life than I could learn in stuffy lecture halls, or so I thought. But his is not a success story."

"Your gambler father taught you this uncanny skill of reading people?"

"Among other skills, yes. But I don't want to talk about me. The topic bores me senseless. I don't want to talk about Brian of the two faces, either, so that leaves the subject of you. Let me guess. You grew up in a neat, white house with a father who was a businessman and a mother who baked sweet biscuits. You went to a proper school, and you were top of your class and a Girl Guide."

"We call them sugar cookies and Girl Scouts. Otherwise you got it about right. Is my ordinary background so evident?"

"To be normal is not to be ordinary," he said softly. "I always envied the lads who lived in real homes and knew—" He stopped and shifted. "Tell me about your mother. Was she beautiful like you?"

Laurie shaded her eyes. "My mother had an overstuffed chair in her bedroom with pink and brown roses on it. I would sit on her lap and she'd read to me for hours—wonderful stories—that's where I first learned about Gypsies."

He smiled wistfully. "And your father?"

"My father bought a cabin on a lakeshore and we spent every weekend there. My parents and my brother and I. We'd swim and fish in summer and ice-skate in winter."

"One can tell, Laurie, that you were loved."

"Why do you say that?"

"There is a certain gentleness in you. It just . . . it shows."

A poignant sadness fell upon her; she couldn't miss the hint of envy in his voice.

He said, "But growing up on trust wouldn't have prepared you for the likes of Brian. Have there been other Brians?"

She stared at him. "Yes. Several."

"I thought so."

"Why? Because I'm naive?"

"No, because you're trusting."

"Not anymore. I learn slowly, but I do learn."

"If it were a better world," he said softly, "you wouldn't have to learn not to trust."

Laurie digested this in silence, while a wren chirped in the branches overhead. "Old wise one," she said.

"I'll own the old part, if I look as old as I feel this morning."

"Eric, I hate to be brutal, but you look like you might expire at any moment. I've seen snowmen who have more color than you. Your head still hurts, doesn't it?"

"I'll admit to having recurring images of your aspirin bottle. I just need a few aspirin and a shower and a bit of rest. After which I'll be more worthy of the company of a lovely lady...just a little time to sleep... perchance to dream...of you in firelight...the way you were last night."

She shook her head, smiling. "Did you know you mumble in your sleep?"

"Only when I'm in pain. Otherwise I only groan. But please, in my absence, will you consider this. Our destinies—yours and mine—were to meet on this island, this bulge out of a cold sea, this isolated dot. Our paths crossed here for a reason. Take a moment to think of this, my lady."

He rose, wincing with discomfort. She handed him his cassette player and headphones, to spare him from having to bend over.

He walked slowly down the slope of meadow toward the cottage.

He is an act, she thought. *He's a player on a stage. Center stage, Act One, Scene Three. Curtain down.* Still, he was amusing, which was probably all he meant to be. Destiny, indeed.

When he was out of sight, Laurie walked to the cliffs that overhung the ocean. Her mind was in a muddle. Brian married? Damn, it was true. The half-crazy, half-Gypsy Englishman was right. All the little jagged pieces dropped perfectly into place, each one cutting, drawing blood as it fell.

But what had she lost? A man who'd lied to her and to a wife. A man she would have left instantly, had she known. One doesn't lose what one never had.

Eric leaped right on it, didn't he? Just threw the truth out like a dagger to her heart. Cruelly.

Or did he do it because hating Brian would assuage the hurt of his leaving? Did Eric know that much about women? About people? Maybe. Damn it, probably. Had he learned that too from his gambling father? Or was it a gift passed down for generations in the hot, restless blood of Gypsies?

ERIC FOUND Jeanne Gunn in the front garden of Dawning Cottage. She straightened from the flower bed when she saw him walk up the path.

"You've the look of a lad in pain."

He nodded. "The next time I have hiccups, I will just down a pint and head off to bed."

"Have you hiccups?"

"Last night I had hiccups at the Red Wolf. I assumed Laurie told you."

"No. Was it important?"

"It nearly got me killed." He thought it interesting that Laurie hadn't mentioned it. "I traded the hiccups for the cracked head, Mrs. Gunn. I'm going to phone my office in London, if you don't mind. I'll make a note of the charges."

"You'd do better resting, from the look of you."

"As soon as I've made a brief call."

Laurie's aspirin bottle was still on the small table in the parlor. Eric downed four tablets without water and went to the telephone in the main hallway, holding his throbbing head.

The wait seemed forever.

"Aquarius Recordings."

Eric's voice was slurred, he knew. "Len, I need you to express-post some tapes."

"Eric? Are you all right? You sound different."

"A little groggy is all, after a bloody awful night."

"Are you working or partying?"

"It's not what you think. I fell and cracked my head.... I've got a roaring headache, but I'll live. I always do."

"That's so, Eric—you can survive anything. What tapes do you want?"

"The subliminal program tapes ... classical music."

"*Which* subliminal program? Cures for insomnia, anger control, or pain relief for your aching head?"

"No, hell, no. The subliminal romance tapes. I don't know what marketing numbers you've given them—"

"What? The Falling-in-Love program? You've found a subject?"

"Right. It's a chance to get some data on what we're marketing. Speed them on up here, will you?"

"How am I supposed to speed anything up beyond the barriers of civilization?"

"Whatever way you have to. Look, the ferry crosses once a day, so you need to get them to the ferry by two o'clock tomorrow."

"Impossible."

"Then send them by air. This is important, Len. I've met a beautiful woman who likes classical music, and there are no distractions in this place. The conditions were made to order."

Len's voice picked up enthusiasm. "I thought you'd have tapes with you."

"I have jazz and listening music, no classical."

"All right. It's done. How's the taping coming?"

"Slow. Bloody rain. I recorded some fine rainstorms, though, before my boots filled with mud."

"Is it raining now?"

"No. Today's fine. Be sure to pay at that end to have the package transported by a Post Office van from Fyfe's Landing to Dawning Cottage. I'm short of cash."

A mild, muffled curse crackled along the phone line. "How about trading jobs, Eric?"

"Face it. I'm better in the field and you're better in the studio. Nothing can change that. Cheerio, Len."

Eric went to the kitchen for a glass of milk, moving as silently as possible so he wouldn't attract the attention of Miss Marion Huckles, who sat in the sunny breakfast room writing in a thick notebook. She sat stiffly, head tilted slightly, feet flat on the floor, the tip of her tongue protruding from tightly closed lips.

He viewed Marion Huckles's scandalous memoirs with great skepticism, believing she could never have been young—not with the deep furls sculpted into her brown-and-salt-and-pepper hair pulled back severely from her face, and the pinched expression—her eyes were like little fishhooks.

They were eyes he tried to avoid, because they caused him great discomfort. Marion's mind was easier to read than any other he'd ever encountered. Her thoughts devoured him and sometimes made him feel as if he had a rash.

Laurie MacDonald's mind—now that was another matter. Eric wished they hadn't had that conversation about trust, considering the fact he planned to use her as an experimental subject without her consent. But it wasn't on a personal level—they were all but strangers. Laurie was astute, self-assured and obviously independent, all of which made her a great subject. And there was that gentleness in her—femininity at its purest and its most mysterious. Her beauty drew him.

It was fortunate for him that Laurie was in the process of clearing another man from her mind. The timing was good. The subliminal messages directing her thoughts to Eric would help her forget the lover who'd betrayed her. Perfect.

Or was it? What was that trash he'd been telling her about truth? A pang of doubt shot through him. He suppressed it immediately. The tapes, after all, might have little effect. They were marketed with impressive claims, not just by his company, but by companies the world over. But the research on the validity of the claims was inconclusive. Results and opinions varied greatly. Some studies showed hypnotic influence, but others didn't back this up. No realistic data, to Eric's knowledge, was available anywhere.

The pain relievers began to work. In the kitchen, he drank a glass of milk. He was less successful in getting back to his room afterward without being seen.

Marion looked up over the rim of her glasses. Her face registered shock at his unshaven appearance, as if it were planned as a personal insult to her. "Oh, are you up?"

"No," he answered. "I'm still asleep."

Her lips drew into a tiny bud. "You have milk on your whiskers."

He wiped his mouth with the back of his hand.

"Like a cat," she added, turning back to her writing.

He hurried toward the stairs.

Eric had the largest and best room in Dawning Cottage. Its windows looked out in the direction of the sea. In a corner was a small fireplace, which he had already used once. Two overstuffed chairs and a small table fitted comfortably in the spacious area opposite the bed.

He undressed, filled the washbasin, and splashed cold water onto his face before he got into bed, willing the comfort of sleep. Sleeping during the day was against all of his principles, except when he had a grueling hangover. Today the ache in his head counted for two grueling hangovers.

He thought of Laurie MacDonald. Everything about courting her smacked of adventure, starting with the fact that she was an American. She was quick-witted, challenging and sensitive. He liked her. It had been tacky of him to lie about having seen the Loch Ness monster, but the situation had called for it at the time.

Eric was amazed that she had never figured out that Brian was married. Miss MacDonald's choice of men must not be too discriminating, he deduced—and that evaluation was encouraging.

Eric stretched full length between the cold sheets, his body still cramped from the harrowing night on the parlor sofa.

"Classical..." he muttered sleepily, with a smile. "Classical you want, pretty lady... classical it is...."

4

THE FRESH SEA AIR was washed with pale sunshine. Exploring the far side of the island, Laurie was still in a state of mild shock over the exhumation of the bones of Brian's lies. Her thrill at seeing the Celtic ceremonial site was so darkened by the cloud of hurt that she could do little more than stand and stare at the circle of narrow, perpendicular stones.

She felt strange vibrations in the area. The sunshine filtered through high branches of a cluster of oak trees. The stones, cold with age, somehow still felt damp in the sunshine. One aging oak stood apart from the others, its leaves whispering dark and terrible secrets of the Druid cult that had practiced sacrifice in its shadow. The spirits of the dead lingered in the quiet, isolated meadow, haunting the moors and the streams.

Allowing the residual evil of this silent place to enter her mind and her body and blend with the ache of resentment over Brian's deceit, Laurie walked about the flowering meadow taking slide photographs. It was almost exactly as she had pictured it, but she hadn't predicted the awareness of the ghosts.

On this, her second day on Lees, Laurie didn't stay long at the standing stones. Fighting the bleak mood, she hurried back to the fleeting warmth of the afternoon sun in the garden at the back of Dawning Cottage.

Stretched out on the patch of green lawn, she lay watching sea gulls play on the wind above her and tried to clear her mind of everything depressing or irritating or otherwise having to do with men. Her eyes closed finally and she drifted.

Like a warm breeze teasing flower petals, music swept over her—a haunting kind of music, almost but not quite familiar. Almost but not quite vapor. . . .

From the shallow slumber she was roused by the presence of Eric Sinclair. She imagined at first, opening her eyes, that the breeze was his breath and the music his voice. He was sprawled on the grass near her, again with his cassette tape player.

Brushing back her shoulder-length hair, she sat up. "I didn't see you there."

He said, "I'm invading your privacy. But an apology would be ludicrous, considering that I'm intruding quite deliberately."

The confession was delivered without the appropriate smile. Laurie answered, "I have no claims on the garden. Are you rested now, Eric? How is your head? I haven't seen even a hint of you since yesterday."

"I drove round to the village to pick up some mail and got delayed at the Red Wolf on the way back last night."

Laurie leaned back on her elbows, gazed up at the overhanging branches and sighed. The leaves formed shadows on themselves, shadows making a pattern in the wind. "What is that music you're playing?"

Eric reached over to turn up the sound. "Light classical medleys. Like it?"

"Yes. It sounds Hungarian. Makes me think of Gypsies."

"What do you think of when you think of Gypsies, Laurie?"

Her smile was dreamy. She allowed herself to grasp the fantasy and dissolve into it. "A camp fire. The music of violins and guitars. The night pitch-black all around the bright glow of the fire. Arm and ankle bracelets of the dancers reflecting gold as they move...."

"There ought to be a moon in that picture," he said.

She nodded. "Sometimes there is a moon."

"A half moon that rises like a full moon. Have you seen it?"

Laurie looked over at him, protecting her eyes from her blowing hair. "A half moon rising? No. Have you?"

"Naturally." His mysterious eyes were riveted on hers. "Since I'm a Gypsy."

"Yes, so you claim. A blue-eyed Gypsy with an English accent and a tape recorder in place of a guitar."

"And a lovely lady at my side. And open sky, and a fair breeze blowing perfume off the moors. What more could any man want?"

For a time they sat in silence, listening to the music.

"You didn't answer about your head," she said finally.

"A collision with a table leg is nothing of consequence. Bumps and slashes are merely the marks of a life well lived."

She straightened, smiling. "What kind of philosophy is that?"

"Only dull men seek the safe life."

Laurie observed him carefully, trying to determine whether or not he believed what he was saying. His eyes were filled with hidden messages, making it hard to judge. "There is a wide space in between dull and reckless, Eric."

His returned gaze held new respect for her. Obviously he liked to be challenged. "I prefer to err on the side of reckless. However this—" he touched the side of his head gingerly "—was a generic accident that could have happened to anybody."

"Yes. Anybody who was sitting with one foot in ice water and one in hot." Laurie cringed. "I apologize, Eric. It was my fault you were hurt."

"Nonsense. It was the fault of the laddie who frightened me off balance. Your cure ultimately worked. Do you see me complaining?"

"You did plenty of complaining that night. But never mind. I'm glad you have such powers of recovery."

The music stopped. She watched him take out the cassette tape, turn it over and slide it back into the machine.

He leaned back lazily and gazed at the sky. "It's going to rain before an hour has passed."

"There's only a slight chill in the air," she challenged. "No sign of rain."

"Ah, but there is a sure sign." He twisted his shoulders as if he were trying to wriggle out of his clothes. "My back itches. My back always itches before it rains, and the way that bloody itch is crawling, it'll be much sooner than I originally predicted."

He turned away, offering the back of his broad shoulders to her. "Please? I hate to be a pest, but . . . please?"

It was easy, even natural for her to reach out to him. Her hands moved with a circular motion over his hard back, outside his shirt. The circles were timed, she came to realize, to the rhythm of the music he was playing.

Laurie experienced a sensation of déjà vu, as if she'd been with him like this before, some time, some place, touching him, her fingertips tingling as if she were absorbing the energy of his body into hers. Impossible, of course, yet touching him made her feel she knew him better than she should.

"Ahh," he breathed with a great sigh of pleasure. "Magic fingers. A little to the left and down."

A shadow fell over them as the sun ducked behind a bank of low, gray clouds that had blown in without warning from over the sea.

Laurie said, "It's suddenly getting cold."

"Don't stop. Your touch is magical."

Hunched over, arms resting on his knees, Eric was all but purring. He'd heard a weather forecast, she thought. The silly business of predicting rain by a back itch was a sneaky way of inviting her touch. Or getting himself a back scratch, whichever was more important to him. She could only smile and acquiesce to the subtle rhythm of the music.

A figure appeared on the stone pathway only a few meters away. How long had she been there? Laurie wondered uneasily. The chiffon scarf Marion wore about her head had long, wide tails that flapped in the wind like wings. The woman stood on the rocky ledge, wings undulating, as though she were ready to fly.

"That music is an intrusion," Marion told him.

Eric straightened to attention and stopped the tape with one swift motion. "How long have you been standing there listening?"

"It's of no consequence how long."

Laurie didn't like the look on Eric's face. He seemed angered that Marion had heard the music.

Marion took a few steps nearer. "That noise upsets the balance of nature."

"Whose nature?" he asked irritably.

"The music wasn't loud," Laurie said. "It must have been hard to hear in the wind."

"Wind is my element!" the other woman declared raising her head and her voice to the rising sea breeze. "I take my inspiration and vigor from the wind. I came out to greet a storm, not to be assaulted by limp parlor music. Your music is an insult to nature's sense of drama. And yes, to mine too."

Eric rose to his feet. "The sky's going to open up. That should be drama enough. Me, I'm for tea. I'll go up and lay a fire in the parlor for Mrs. Gunn."

He offered Laurie his hand, and as she rose, their eyes met and held, until she self-consciously glanced away. "Marion," Laurie said. "Are you coming in for tea? You're going to get soaked out here."

"I shall be vitalized by the storm. Renewed by wind, the secret of my inner strength. The storm is my music!"

Eric urged Laurie toward the cottage. Her skirt blew against her legs, and a few, flying raindrops stung her cheeks. He closed the door against the wind and set his recorder in the hallway by the foot of the stairs.

"The image of a soaking-wet Marion isn't something I particularly relish," he said in the sitting room while he was lighting the fire.

Through the lace-curtained window they saw Marion duck under trees at the edge of the path, not far from the front entrance to the cottage. It looked as though she was heading in out of the rain, after all. Was this bravado over the storm—and everything else about her—no more than a badly done act? Laurie expected another sarcastic comment from Eric about Marion's sneaking inside after her performance, but he said nothing.

Other things were on his mind. Laurie had already got the message that *she* was on his mind.

Today he looked at her differently, but the difference was hard to define. Had something in his eyes softened her suspicions and stimulated her curiosity? His eyes? His voice? His manner?

The room warmed quickly. Laurie took off her red cardigan and curled in a chair, conscious of Eric's eyes on the curves of her body under the silk blouse. She felt a little giddy and blamed it on Eric's blue eyes.

Who was he, really?

He was a man of contradictions. Sometimes, when he smiled, his eyes did not. Sometimes, when the light shone on his scar and his eyes were icy pale, he looked almost wicked. Other times his voice would come soft and sad, as if he hurt somewhere deep inside.

He talked of his past without emotion, as if it weren't quite real. Either he was fabricating, or he had never come to terms with his own identity. Laurie sensed something wrong. Probably he was playing games, covering his real identity with lies.

When she saw him looking at her though, in rare unguarded moments, Laurie felt the vibrations all through her body. The glances were not deliberate, but their effect was unnerving. Eric was an intensely sensual man seeing her as a woman.

Jeanne Gunn brought tea. The sky darkened until all the lamps in the parlor were on. Twenty minutes later Marion came in, still wearing the flowing, gray chiffon scarf about her hair and looking wildly windblown. Eric excused himself quietly. They could hear his footsteps grow softer as he ascended the stairs.

The peat fire sizzled and steamed in its own sweet aroma. Rain began to slash at the window. The rockers of Mrs. Gunn's chair creaked with a steady rhythm as she sat at her knitting, her teacup beside her, a smile on her face while she told stories of ghosts who walked the moors. Laurie listened in fascination, for many of the local legends had their obscure beginnings far back in Celtic superstitions.

This afternoon, however, her concentration was not fully on Jeanne's stories. With one ear tuned to the sounds of the storm, Laurie wondered if Eric had been teasing her about being able to predict rain with an itching back. After all, rain was quite predictable on this sea-splashed Scottish island.

It was impossible to tell when the Gypsy man was serious and when he wasn't.

DINNER AT DAWNING COTTAGE was not an elaborate affair. The fare was hearty and simple, always beef or lamb with fresh vegetables. Bread and pastries were baked fresh every day. Mrs. Gunn set a table for four, expecting her guests to dine together at eight o'clock sharp.

Somewhat to Laurie's surprise, Eric showed up in the dining room this night, and on time, dressed for dinner in a forest-green sport coat with leather on the sleeves. He wore a tie as custom dictated, even in this remote outreach of civilization. His collar was not buttoned under the tie knot, however, and his hair was not carefully combed. Perhaps he had decided to stay in because of the storm. The road between Dawning and the Red Wolf would turn quickly to mud in the pooling of the steady fall of rain.

Laurie sensed the tenseness in the dining room. If the wind had revitalized Marion this afternoon, the renewal wasn't evident. She sat as stiffly as ever, her eyes moving from Jeanne to Laurie and generally avoiding Eric. He seemed preoccupied and distant.

"More rain to slow up your work," Jeanne Gunn said as she poured Burgundy into Eric's glass.

"I don't mind it as much as I pretend," he answered. "It gives me an excuse to stay out of London."

"And what, pray tell us," Marion said as she passed across a dish of buttered turnips, "do you dislike about London?"

He accepted the dish and served himself. "Noise. When people are bombarded with industrial sounds, they themselves tend to become machines."

"People become machines? What sort of ridiculous theory is that now?"

"It's a fact. They wake up to the sound of an alarm, eat at the signal of a microwave beep, drive to the commands of whistles, horns and lights—"

"Spare us having to go through an entire work day."

"All right, we'll skip to the evening of television programming, the end of which is the command to retire."

"Eric has a point," Mrs. Gunn observed.

Marion raised one eyebrow. "Eric's point has a dull edge."

He laughed wickedly, but to Laurie's relief, he did not dignify Marion's dangerous remark with a retort.

Jeanne Gunn looked from one guest to another. "I find it interesting that none of you is here on holiday, but doing work of one sort or another... Eric his recording, Marion her book, and Laurie the Celtic research."

"My project is less related to work than personal interest," Laurie told her.

Marion was sprinkling salt onto her food by cautiously tapping the side of the crystal saltshaker with her finger. She set the shaker down and looked at each of the others in turn. "I have news. In actual fact, very exciting news."

The tone of her voice expressed the exaggerated control of a child feigning nonchalance in the adult world. Their full attention fell upon her.

Savoring the moment, Marion dabbed the edges of her mouth ceremoniously, straightened and slipped on a rehearsed smile. "A publisher is interested in my book. He is going to meet me."

The announcement was met with silence. All eyes were on her and not one glance shifted. They didn't trust themselves to glance at each other.

"That's wonderful!" Laurie exclaimed at last.

"It's incredible," Eric commented, meaning it.

Marion frowned at him. "It is the publisher's gain, and he knows it. However, admittedly, this gruesome business of breaking into the publishing world can be trying. Odd as it seems, it has not been easy finding a reputable publisher willing to offer a fair contract."

"Is everything done and dusted then?" Eric asked, his head cocked sideways and his brow knitted. He knew his blue eyes were too full of skepticism to look at her.

"Not quite. I received a letter. It seems publishing a book like mine from an . . . unknown, as they call it, would involve a publicity tour. Considering the rather scandalous nature of the book, they want to meet me, see who I am and how I live now in my semiretirement, as it were."

Laurie cut into her lamb chop. "Where do you live?"

"At the moment, here."

Jeanne Gunn leaned forward, blinking behind her glasses. "Are you saying a publisher is coming here?"

The author smiled and smoothed the skirt of her floral print rayon dress. "Yes. Isn't it marvelous?"

"When?"

"I'm not sure. A few days. You have got another room."

"Yes." The hostess looked uneasy.

"You will keep the room free, won't you? They will let me know very soon. Oh, it will be grand! It's lovely here. Just the sort of place a lady escaping the beams and bruises of a much-lived past can escape into reminiscence."

Beams and bruises? Good heavens! Laurie knew her discomfort was shared by Eric and Jeanne Gunn. A publisher had undoubtedly taken the work at face value and expected to find a sultry vamp, around whom he could launch a bawdy publicity campaign. He was in for the shock of his life. No good could come of this. Marion's marvelous news put a damper on the evening for everyone but Marion.

Mischief sparkled in Eric's blue eyes. "To bring a publisher up to the Hebrides rather than asking you to London...quite a feat, that. Perhaps this book of yours is too hot to handle."

"Perhaps it is," she answered.

"Based on your own life, you've said. Your own past."

She sipped her tea coolly. "My memoirs, yes."

His brows rose in awe. "You've come through it all so unscarred."

Her eyes narrowed. She seemed unsure if she had been insulted, but in case she had been, it was necessary to jab back. "My scars are not the kind that show. Unlike you. We ought to talk about your past for once, Mr. Sinclair. I'm sure you have your share of dark, well-kept secrets. Maybe you'd like to tell us about the origin of that scar on your chin, for instance. The result of a fight, isn't it?"

He was slow to answer. His forefinger followed the narrow line of the four-inch scar. "It's a rather personal subject."

"Fights are hardly subtle. As to the cause of the fray...we're all friends here. What are you afraid of?"

He glanced at Laurie, who had stopped eating. Mrs. Gunn was at full attention, knowing Eric wasn't likely to back down from Marion's challenge.

"Well?" she goaded.

"I was cut with a knife," he admitted. He focused his attention on the wineglass.

"Don't stop there, please," Jeanne begged.

He continued to touch the scar. "Not much of a fight, if you want the truth. When I was working on the wharves at Liverpool I was jumped by three thugs. I fought back, but I was no match for them. One was holding me when another came at me with a knife. If I hadn't managed to kick the blackguard where it hurt most, he'd have slashed my throat instead of my jaw. Probably the only reason I'm alive to tell it is that the yelling brought some sailors out of the shadows and the thugs tore off. They got my pay, such as it was. My wound was stitched up by a woman who ran a brothel near the pier." Suddenly Eric remembered his meal and proceeded to finish the last two bites. "I was eleven years old at the time."

All three women gasped. Surely, Laurie thought, this couldn't be true! He was playing a game with Marion. Yet at some point in his narrative she had seen the mischief in his eyes change into the blank gaze he used to conceal pain. His voice was without emotion, his body relaxed. But the clouds that formed in his eyes were giveaways. With a sinking in her stomach, Laurie knew the story was true.

Whether or not the other two women saw the clouds and also knew, Laurie couldn't be sure. Whether or not he even intended to be believed, she couldn't tell, either.

He was so full of games and stories and mysteries that it was hard to fathom who the real man was. He wanted it that way.

He was a man with secrets.

Challenged in a game, Eric had just proven he would always play. . . and win.

Marion was staring at him. He pretended not to notice. Laurie, however, did notice, and was horrified by what she saw. Lust. And adoration as strong as any Laurie had ever seen. No wonder Marion had to constantly goad him; it was her only protection from herself. Laurie wondered if Eric knew.

Of course he knew. Nothing escaped him.

"You had a strange childhood," Jeanne Gunn said softly.

"It had its strong points." Eric smiled with his lips, not his eyes. "Never again, after that day, was anybody able to take me by surprise, or. . ." He paused and let his voice fade. Whatever he'd begun, he'd changed his mind about saying.

"Or what?" Laurie prodded. "Or take you in a fight?"

His smiled broadened. "Right."

"It's a horrible story," Marion said.

"You asked me."

"Yes, I suppose I did."

"Hell, it was a long time ago. Yesterday no longer exists—if it ever existed at all."

Marion was alert. "What is that supposed to mean?"

Mrs. Gunn rose swiftly. "I've baked a cherry pie for dessert. Shall we have it in the parlor by the fire? This room is too cold with the rain. I'm feeling the dampness in my knees."

"Let me help you," Laurie offered.

"None for me, thanks," Eric said, rising at the same time Laurie did. "I've got some work to do upstairs."

"And skip the Drambuie?" Jeanne asked.

His head is aching and he doesn't want to admit it, Laurie thought. In fact, he'd probably deny it if she asked. She suspected his recovery from the head blow was not as complete as he would have them believe. He'd seemed distracted during dinner. Restless.

Laurie felt restless, too.

She sat in the cozy room across from the other two women, reading. Jeanne was reading also, and Marion was scribbling in her notebook, constantly adjusting her glasses, which would slide back down her nose immediately. She had the annoying habit of constantly tapping the pen against the paper.

Above the sound of the ticking of Marion's pen, the wind was scraping a wet tree branch against the window glass. The loneliness of this faraway island lived in the silence of the room. Had it not been for that million-to-one sighting of a monster most of the world didn't believe existed, Brian would be with her tonight, and she would be unaware of the loneliness. Brian probably expected a reconciliation when she returned home. The next surprise would be his.

Strange how little remained of Brian in her heart besides the anger. Or maybe not so strange, with Eric Sinclair stubbornly occupying her thoughts tonight. That beautiful music he had played in the garden . . .

Reading was impossible. She closed the book and set it down. "If you'll excuse me . . ."

Marion yawned noisily and tucked her notebook under her arm. "Me, too. I've gone past my usual bedtime, because I keep thinking of . . . you know, the publisher who wants my book. I'm outlining a sequel."

She accompanied Laurie up the wide stairway, talking incessantly until they parted company in the square upper hallway and went to their respective bedrooms.

Solitude mixed with cold was lonelier still. Laurie slipped into her flannel nightgown and curled up in bed, quilts pulled to her chin. She made sketches of the standing stones she'd seen today, trying to theorize on their unusual positioning. They appeared to form a triangle rather than the circle every book described. While sketching, her eyelids grew heavy. Beginning to doze, she heard the music again.

Eric's music. The same, haunting, Gypsy music he had played this afternoon in the garden was drifting into her bedroom. He must play music all the time, she thought dreamily as she settled back and listened, eyes closed, allowing the music to settle over her like a gentle mist. The picture of Gypsies came to her again. This time she saw Eric as one of them. He was playing a guitar in the light of a bright half moon, and the firelight was shining in his sensuous eyes. For a long time she lay floating on the music in the warmth of her bed.

She didn't sleep. In fact, the music seemed to have the opposite effect; it made her dreamy, but it also made her strangely restless. Extremely restless. She wondered what Eric was doing in his room. Had he fallen asleep in there? Or was he working?

She had to get up, leave the warmth. Not to check on Eric, she told herself, but because the bathroom was on the opposite side of the hallway. Shivering, she was slipping on warm socks when the music suddenly stopped and she heard loud voices, and her own name, in the hall.

Laurie opened the door to find Marion in a purple robe and Eric in jeans and a sweater, both standing immediately outside her door. Marion's hair was flying in all directions and she was waving her arms. Eric was holding his tape recorder, looking frighteningly angry.

Marion's voice crackled and shrieked. "Eric Sinclair, what is the meaning of this?"

5

LAURIE STEPPED into the hall. "What's going on?"

"That's what I'd like to know." Marion scowled, hands on her hips. "Eric is playing music out here in the middle of the night, deliberately trying to keep us awake."

"I thought you'd be asleep, Marion," he answered defensively. "I didn't think you'd hear it."

"Oh really? And Laurie? You set that blessed machine right outside Laurie's door!"

"You did what?" Laurie asked.

He glared at his accuser, then turned to Laurie. "Hell, I was serenading you, that's all. The palace guard here happened to venture into the hall."

"You did what?" Laurie repeated.

Marion's face was by now the color of her purple robe. She shifted her weight from one foot to the other. "I came out to ask Eric to turn down the music in his room, and I find this...tape recorder *in* the hall, *thrust* against your door."

"You couldn't have heard the music," he insisted.

"I could and I did!"

Whether or not Marion had heard the music seemed to be a great issue for Eric. The question why it bothered him flitted through Laurie's mind, but she was curiously pleased by his romantic gesture.

"Did you say...serenade?" Laurie inquired.

His hands raised in a helpless gesture. "You like my music. I felt like sharing it. Must I have a reason?"

She gazed at him. "The truth is, I was enjoying it. I thought it was coming through the wall."

"We were not *all* enjoying it," Marion said in an injured voice. She, too, seemed more upset than the matter called for. Glaring at Eric, she mumbled, "Adolescent behavior, don't you think?" before she turned abruptly and shot back into her bedroom, her loose slippers slapping against the floor.

Eric turned to Laurie. "Adolescent behavior? Me?"

She laughed softly. "Absurd. How were you... uh...sharing this, if I might ask? Were you sitting out here on the cold floor or did you have your door open?"

"I was in my room keeping an eye on my bait, ready to spring when you came out to investigate. Part two of the plan was to invite you into my wee lair for a nip of brandy. And if by chance you didn't appear, then I'd comfort myself with knowing that the same music played us both to sleep tonight."

"You'd fall asleep with your door wide open?"

"Why not? I've nothing to hide."

Laurie glanced toward Marion's room. "In that case, I'll accept your offer for a nip of brandy. If only because—"

"You're cold," he said.

"I should have brought a warm robe. I haven't a robe."

"I remember very well. Ah, but there's a fireplace in my room. The fire isn't burning at the moment, but I can light it."

"Oh, no, not this late. A blanket over my shoulders will do fine. I won't stay very long."

By the time she had pulled a blanket from her bed and run a brush quickly through her hair, Eric had poured two snifters of brandy in his room and was waiting for her.

She paused in his open doorway before she entered. Neither made a move to close the door behind her. In silence he handed her the glass. His music was playing again, softly filling the room.

"I look ridiculous," she said.

"I beg to disagree."

"Then you're kind. Your room is very nice with the fireplace."

"This one was vacant when I came. We can exchange rooms, if you like."

"Good heavens, no. You need the space because you have all your work set up in here." Electronic recording equipment was set here and there about the room. The small desk and table held notebooks and papers and tapes. "What are you working on?"

"Market reports and expenses and proposals for new taping projects. Being in the field, as it were, doesn't let me escape from the less pleasant aspects of the business world. My partner and I own a small, but expanding, recording company."

She sat in one of the comfortable chairs and curled her stockinged feet under her. "I can't picture you confined to an office building."

"It's not a picture you'd see very often. I use every excuse I can conjure up to stay out of the office. I don't mind the studio work in doses, but I couldn't take a steady diet of it. I need fresh air."

"Then it's true you don't mind the rain that delays your work."

He poured himself a second drink. "I must pretend to mind it to my partner, but of course I don't. Especially now that I've met you. Rain delays your project, too, and nothing could please me more. It will still be raining tomorrow. It will drizzle all night."

"Your back is still itching?"

"Abominably."

"Maybe you're allergic to wool. Ever think of that?"

"I have, yes. Wet sheep make me sneeze. Could there be a correlation, do you think?"

Laurie's eyes scanned his silhouette. The lamplight at his back formed a glow around his body. He was so perfectly built. Husky and solid. Big and somehow wild. She could picture him fighting. Strangely she could picture him with the sun in his eyes and the moon at his back—both at the same time. Was he somehow trying to confuse her?

"Eric . . ." she began, and paused.

"What?"

"Eric . . . how much of you is fraudulent?"

"What does that mean?"

"How much of you is fraught with fraudulence?"

He grinned. "Do you want a percentage?"

"If you had to give it a percentage . . . how high?"

"I suppose the figure fluctuates."

"Depending on what?"

"Obviously on who I'm with."

"I see...." She swirled the liquid in her glass and watched the patterns of the swirls for a time. "You don't even try to deny that you're...well...rather fraudlike."

"What? Froglike?"

"No! Fraud. Maybe that word is too strong, but you just admitted you're not always to be believed."

He cringed visibly. "What's the matter, Laurie? Don't you like me?"

"Of course I like you. I just get the feeling that something isn't quite right. Oh, it's your mischief, I suppose. Everyone says you have the ways of a tinker about you. And I believed there were no more Scottish Gypsies left."

"Sure there are tinkers left. Not in caravans, but..." He rubbed his chin, over the scar. "Look. All right, Laurie, I'll admit to a lady of your superior intelligence that sometimes I can be...fraudlike. But I see life...all of it...as a game. People who don't see life as a game are the victims of those who do. I didn't make the rules, but I play by them. My philosophy is that life is to be enjoyed, not to be suffered through."

"Your story at dinner about your scar. Is it true?"

"I'm afraid so."

"You worked on the docks at age eleven? Loading cargo?"

"I was too small to load cargo. I worked the docks on paydays as a pickpocket."

She gasped. "That can't be true!"

"Seeing the look on your face, I wish it weren't true. But take faith, fair lass, I don't still practice the art."

"But you *could*. If you wanted."

"I'd be a bit rusty." He studied her. "Laurie, I could lie to you about what I am, but what would be the point? Look. We all just find ourselves at a spot on earth, in a spot of time and we look around and say, 'This is the world, this is life,' and we proceed to do the best we can with it. In the beginning there aren't many choices. The choices, if they come at all, come later."

"Yes. Much later."

He smiled softly. "I'm glad you made the choice to come into my room tonight."

"I've never been invited more eloquently—with a musical serenade outside my door."

"And I've never wished for someone's company enough to resort to such desperate tactics. But what could I do? You have no balcony for me to climb."

His words set off an echo in her head. *Never*, he had said. Never wished for someone's company this much? A man like this? With charm like this? Who looked like this? It had to be a lie. She made a conscious choice to believe the lie. Because she wanted to.

The haunting music continued to play. Something about Eric drew her to him in a way she had never before been drawn to a man. A small voice inside her tried to fight the attraction by marching through her head, reciting a bitter chronicle of past events from Brian on back, but the small voice was crying against a storm. All Laurie could hear was the music and Eric's deep, sensual, English accent.

When he moved nearer to replace her drink, Laurie caught the scent of his cologne for the first time. Had he put it on tonight for her?

She said, "It's extremely manipulative of you to keep playing that music."

He looked startled. "What do you mean?"

"You know that whenever I hear it for the rest of my life I'll think of you. That's what you want, isn't it?"

He brushed her cheek lightly with his lips. "I want your thoughts of me always to be pleasant."

The hint of his kiss was so rakish that she began to question her own mixed emotions. "Eric . . . why do I have an awful feeling we're being watched?"

"Who would be watching us?"

"I don't know. I just have this prickling sense of something wrong, something happening around us that we don't know about."

He sat back. "There are spirits on this island. The old spirits, still here. Perhaps you're feeling the presence of the nature spirits."

"Surely you don't believe in them."

"Of course I do."

"You do?"

"I always have."

"But . . . why?"

He smiled. "Because I want to. I like the earth spirits. The mean ones keep me in line and the gentle ones sing me to sleep. It's just them. No one else is watching."

She remained unconvinced.

"Shall I close the door?" he asked.

"No. I must go back to my room. It's getting late."

Eric snapped his fingernail against the side of his glass repeatedly, creating tiny, hollow clicks. "What is really bothering you? Me?"

"I don't know. I honestly don't know." She wondered if he was serious about believing in the pagan spirits worshiped by the ancients. She wondered if he was serious about anything. But she was sure that something strange was happening and had no idea what it was.

When she saw herself reflected in his eyes, she wanted to believe in him. He looked at her as no man ever had—with curiosity, awe, admiration—and yet in the dead center of his eyes was a blank spot that held secrets. Maybe little secrets. Maybe terrible secrets. She sensed some kind of danger in Eric Sinclair. And yet she liked him far too much. Maybe that was what was scaring her.

He didn't urge her to stay longer when she began to shuffle to the door, tugging at the blanket to keep it from sliding from her shoulders, but he took her hand, raised it gently to his lips and kissed her fingers lightly. He allowed her hand to brush his cheek. The bristle of his beard was enough to send a tremor through her body. His touch threatened to unravel her completely.

He walked her the few steps through the wide hallway to her room. "Laurie, something has been bothering me. I was insensitive about pointing out to you that your...uh...your travel companion was a less than honorable man. Abruptly, like that. It wasn't a kind thing for me to do."

"On the contrary. It was an act of mercy. My world is better for it."

"So is mine, if it meant your loyalties were diffused. Although I swear that wasn't my motive."

"I know."

He touched her cheek so lightly that his fingers felt like feathers. "You're a lovely lady. You deserve better than him."

"I know." She met his eyes.

He leaned over and kissed her forehead. "Good night. Sleep well."

SLEEP, she demanded of herself as she lay in bed with the thick quilts pulled up to her chin. The room was dark, even darker than the cloud-covered night sky. And the darkness was filled with his music. . . .

It wasn't coming from under the door, surely. The notes must be seeping through the wall. Or was she only imagining? The music was a part of Eric, and it was almost becoming a part of her.

She allowed herself the luxury of thinking about the man who slept on the other side of the wall . . . his unreadable eyes closed now. She tried to picture him as the tough kid he once was, a child without a childhood, but she couldn't think of the child, only of the man. Something about the man frightened her. Laurie fell into the down of sleep, thinking that it was already too late to reflect on the fear.

IN THE GRAY CHILL of morning, she opened the curtains to the sight of dripping skies. He'd been right about the rain. When she crossed the hall to the bathroom, Eric's door was closed and there was no sound from within. She showered quickly, dressed in woolen slacks and a sweater and went downstairs to breakfast.

Marion, seated at her private breakfast spot by the window, gave Laurie a curious glance. Jeanne Gunn set down her teacup and greeted her. Eric was nowhere in sight.

Laurie helped herself to juice and oatmeal from the sideboard and sat down at the table across from Jeanne, who was pouring a cup of tea for her guest and another for herself.

"They're Scottish skies this morning, they are," Mrs. Gunn said. "And wheen clouds moving in. 'Tis a gloomy prospect for all but fish and the wee seeds in my garden."

Across the room Marion sat posed with pen in hand, her notebook on the table beside her china teacup. "I find inspiration in the gloom. It reminds me of a man I met on the Côte d'Azur. We met in the rain. We made love in a field of lavender that reflected the lavender of his eyes. We said goodbye in the rain . . . rain and tears mingling together in a pool of lavender. . . ." She closed her eyes. "Ah, yes, I find inspiration in the gloom."

Laurie was afraid to look at Jeanne in the deathlike silence that followed this recital. Mrs. Gunn clinked her cup onto the saucer. "How will you have your eggs this fine, damp morning, Laurie?"

"Uh . . . easy over," she answered, blinking her way back from the French fields of lavender to the harsh actuality of breakfast.

The author, seated at her private table, bent once more to her rain-inspired work. Laurie sat gazing through the window, past garden colors so bright the drizzle could not subdue them and out to the green hillsides beyond. No sheep were on the moors; they must have come in to shelter. *It is so beautiful here*, she thought, *even in the rain.* Large drops streaked the window glass, forming prisms in reflections of light.

Soon her hostess set a breakfast plate before her, saying, "The roads south to the standing stones will be too muddy to travel over."

"I was afraid of that. And the road across the meadow would be very soggy."

"Aye. It's one good soak we're having. There'll be mean clouds from seaward, mark my words."

The breakfast was hot and delicious—fresh farm eggs, a pork chop and toasted homemade bread. Laurie ate in silence for a full minute. "Have you seen Eric this morning?"

"Not a breath nor a peep. He wouldn't have got up early to record, as he usually does. Not in this weather. So I take it he's still in his bed, snoozing away a fine morning."

"Ambition isn't one of his stronger points," Marion muttered from across the room, not raising her head from her book.

Laurie bristled, but said nothing. It wasn't up to her to defend him, but Marion never missed the slightest chance to take a dig at him. She consistently overreacted to the very mention of his name. Eric must threaten Marion in some way.

Jeanne Gunn scowled at Marion as one would look at a trying child, then turned her eyes back to the younger woman. "Do you hear the foghorn?"

"Yes. Such a lonely sound. Surely no fishermen are out today."

"They probably are, because the wind has tamed."

She supposed Eric had recorded the haunting, wistful sound of the foghorn. Maybe he was out there now; who could guess about him?

A LOW FIRE burned in the parlor. The air was sweet with the smell of Jeanne's freshly baked cinnamon tarts. Laurie buried herself in her books on Celtic customs and mythology of the British Isles—accounts of human sacrifice and dark magic that made her shudder. So little of the Druids was known, none of their doctrines ever written down. The magical forces that had dominated their world could be felt on this island. Spells, legends, were part of history here, along with their spirits of nature—the same spirits Eric professed to believe in. Druid bards could put spells on people with their music. . . .

Interesting, she thought, that she and Eric liked the same music. Even now it swam softly in her head.

Restlessness fell in the sound of rain and soaked through the stories of Druidic magic. Marion had come into the room and sat down across from her, writing as usual and tapping her pen and making strange noises in her throat.

Laurie set aside the book, rose and went to the window.

"Looking for him?" The voice came unexpectedly out of the silence behind her.

Laurie turned. "What?"

Marion didn't look up from her notebook. "His little hall concert might have been amusing last night if I hadn't been trying to sleep. That music. . .it does strange things to a person, I swear it does. It made me feel quite restless. Eric was making a blatant pass at you. I hope you didn't fall for it."

Facing the window again, Laurie answered, "I feel like an overripe apple falling from an apple tree."

"Good Lord. How could you? His cunning games didn't work on *me*." Marion's voice became husky. "But then, of course I'm more experienced."

"Of course," Laurie conceded, moving away from the window and toward the door.

"Where are you going? To look for him?"

"I'm going to wash my hair or something." Anything, just to get out of here, she thought.

"Be careful, Laurie. Be very careful."

"Be careful washing my hair?"

"You know perfectly well what I mean. Be careful of him. The man is quite untrustworthy. Quite lowborn. You heard him admit as much."

Laurie turned back, frowning.

Marion, pale in the glow of the lamplight, looked up and confided in a near whisper, "I've heard talk . . . rumors."

"What rumors?"

Leaning forward, the older woman rasped, "He's a Gypsy in disguise."

"In disguise as what?"

Marion sputtered. "In disguise as . . . as an ordinary man."

"There's nothing ordinary about Eric Sinclair," Laurie told her and smiled. She left the room, closing the door solidly behind her so none of the heat would escape into the chilly hallway.

The house was so quiet it was eerie. No sign of Jeanne Gunn, nor of Eric. Laurie climbed the stairs to her room. His door was still closed. If he was in there working, he was certainly quiet about it.

She had decided to drive down into the village at the ferry landing. Fighting bad roads would be preferable to staying in the cottage with Marion and her melodrama.

In her room a bright yellow paper was taped in the center of her mirror.

L.M.
Take leave of this place, it's worse than haunted.
I'm at the Red Wolf, waiting for you. Why aren't you here yet?

E.

Worse than haunted was right. The tavern would be as lively as a carnival, and he was waiting for her, knowing she'd come. Not just to escape Dawning Cottage, but to be with him. Anticipation of seeing Eric was like waiting for a ride on a merry-go-round, going nowhere, but enjoying the fun of the ride. She hadn't admitted how much she wanted to be with him, to hear his voice, to touch him, but the pull was too strong to deny any longer. She had fallen under his spell.

Laurie slid the note into her pocket, touched up her makeup, dabbed on perfume and took her raincoat and umbrella from the closet.

How did Eric leave without being heard or seen? she wondered as she hurried down the steps to the front door. If she was lucky, she, too, could sneak out with-

out being caught and questioned about where she was
going and why.

Because of the steady rain, the Red Wolf was stirring
with people like Eric and herself, who had been driven
to shelter. Stomping mud from her boots, Laurie
opened the door to loud voices and laughter, remembering the first time she stood on this threshold—three
days ago and forever ago, back in the days when Brian
was still classified as human, and the upside-down man
in the tavern was a weird, eccentric stranger, nothing
more.

He was not at the bar. Her eyes, scanning the room,
were drawn to a splash of pink at a corner table. Eric,
in a shirt of sherbet pink, sat playing cards with four
other men. All appeared to be deeply absorbed in the
game. All, that is, but Eric, who glanced up at her and
winked without moving an inch.

The shirt was distracting. First by its outrageous
color, secondly by the way he wore it, open in front,
revealing the thick, dark hair on his chest, the sleeves
rolled to his elbows.

Aware of eyes on her, Laurie made her way to the bar
and sat down. Some of the people in here would remember her as the woman whose hiccup cure back-
fired and caused a man to be nearly killed. The smiles
were friendly, however. The mood of the place was as
gregarious as before.

She ordered a beer. If she turned slightly, she could
see the card game in the corner. A few others were
watching it, too. Some pound notes were piled in the
center of the table.

"I dinna want to take yer money," one of the men was saying.

"Make your bet, Marnoch," Eric muttered.

While the other players fidgeted, Laurie noted that Eric sat as still as a statue. Only his eyes moved, and fixed hard on each of his opponents in turn, before he moved his gaze on to the next.

These men don't have a chance against him, Laurie thought.

She was right. One by one his opponents folded. A hefty, bearded man, the one called Marnoch, red in the face, got to his feet. "Ach, we shoulda heard the wailin' of tinker pipes when you marched in, Sinclair. It's true, right enough, you've got a tinker's quick hand."

"Tinker, hell. My blood is English," he countered mildly. "And the game was your idea, not mine."

"Of that I'm no so sure, thinkin' back." The big man slung his hands into his empty pockets. "Me, I'm for the road."

"The road is two ruts full of mud," Eric said. "Lay on a smile, mate, and have a round on me. Hell, have three rounds on me, all you worthy mates. I can afford it." He motioned to the bartender to bring ale. Immediately the mood lightened as it became clear that the Englishman intended to leave the tavern with his pockets no fuller than when he came.

When Eric looked toward Laurie, his smile faded. By now she was flanked on two sides by local men vying for her attention. A look that passed over his face told her this situation was unacceptable. He was on his feet at once, crossing the room, oblivious to the many distractions in between them—people talking to him, raising their glasses, instigating another poker game. He seemed to hear none of it. He was on his way to her.

Laurie's heart began to pound, not from fear, but from excitement. Eric was wearing jeans that hugged his thighs and emphasized the sway of his hips as he walked. His shoulder and chest muscles bulged under the fabric of his shirt. Ale spilled over the edge of the glass mug as he walked, but he clearly didn't notice, because his eyes were on the men who stood beside Laurie.

By the time he reached her side, they had backed away. He moved in beside her, brushing his shoulder against hers, a signal of possession that he knew would not be missed. Then the smile returned to his face.

"How do you do it?" she whispered to him when the noise had resumed around them.

"Do what?"

"You frighten people with your eyes."

"These eyes? That look on you with admiration? You've never feared them for a second."

"Not me," she lied. "Other people. Men."

"Men who have designs on my lady are in danger."

She laughed. "Your lady? Who might she be?"

"Don't speak lightly of a serious matter, Laurie. My heart is fragile."

"What are you talking about?"

He looked down at her. "I see myself in your eyes. I did last night. I do now. You're turning me inside out with your beauty and your . . . those . . . thoughts!"

She stared at him through the thick smoke of the ⌐n. In all the noise around them she could hear no t his.

He whispered, "I can read minds, remember?"

He wasn't joking and she knew it. Cold shivers turning warm, turning hot, coursed down her spine. Her hand froze to the handle of the mug she held.

"And what," she managed finally, "exactly what do you read in my mind?"

He hesitated and refused to answer.

With her nails digging involuntarily into the flesh of his arm, she prodded, "What do you read?"

He stared her down, unblinking, through immeasurable suspended time.

"Your thoughts are me, Laurie. You desperately want me."

6

"*WHAT?*" Laurie gasped.

Half smiling, half frowning, he turned away, as though there were other messages in her eyes he preferred not to see. "Look, it . . . it's mutual. It's one of those lightning-bolt strikes that neither of us can control."

Laurie reeled. He stood here, calmly telling her he could not control his wanting her and assumed she felt the same. Mutual, he said. Images shot through her mind like flashes in a storm, images of their bodies close . . . and closer. Laurie's knees went weak, her stomach churned, she fought for control of her voice and her frantic emotions. "You're completely mad."

Eric took a long drink from his mug. "So I read your thoughts. I can pretend I don't, if you prefer. I can pretend I don't, so we can play the proper social game."

"A game, is it?" she asked, although she needn't have. She knew perfectly well what he meant.

And he knew she knew. "We can make all the proper ceremonial moves like a couple of peafowl at mating season. I can strut about showing off my feathers and you can pretend you're not impressed."

"Too late. You've already eliminated that option with ⸰r shocking insolence. Honestly, Eric, this minute I ⸰n't find it too difficult to hate you."

"You'd find it easier to love me."

His closeness, sometimes touching, distracted in a way that embarrassed her. His mind-reading gift was actually becoming believable, and it incensed her.

"Wait," she protested. "Let's not be so free with throwing words around. You used the word love, and I don't—"

"Absolutely."

Laurie brushed her hair from her shoulders. "How can you bring that word into the most carnal conversation that ever existed?"

"It's not carnal."

Ignoring the denial, she leaned closer and whispered, "And I'm shocked. Last night you were so *gentlemanly!*"

"Gentlemen fall in love like everybody else. I was awake all night after you left my room. Did you sleep?"

"Yes," she answered quickly, neglecting to add *and dreamed of you the whole damn night.*

He led her aside to a spot against the wall, where it was more private.

"I didn't mean to make you mad. Forgive me. Sometimes I forget that things I hear weren't said aloud. I forget you didn't say them with your voice and I forget you don't know I've heard them."

She pulled a face. "Oh, please. Just how gullible do you think I am?"

A cloud of sadness settled in his eyes. The sadness was genuine and it confused her.

Silence came between them. From the midst of the tavern noise in the background they heard someone call Eric's name.

"A pull o' ale," a man was saying. "And we'll have another game. Come on, Eric. There's three laddies here will have a go at ye."

"A bit later," he answered.

Grumbling ensued.

"I'll stand the lads a pint in the meantime," Eric said to appease them. He looked back at Laurie. The strange sadness had not gone.

"Let's go where we can be alone," he said.

She stood, consumed by agitation. Bewilderment. Her heart pounded with betrayal—her own heart betraying her—beating with wild excitement at the nearness of him. In anticipation of him. And he knew it. *He knew it.*

She heard her own voice weakly protest, "It's raining. . . ."

His smile was slow, tender. "And everybody is crowded under shelter at Dawning Cottage or here. Never fear. I know a place where we can be alone. We might get a bit wet en route, but we're not without weatherproof gear." He took her hand. "Let's go. If the smoke in this room gets any worse, I won't be able to see those questions in your eyes."

HE REVERSED THE CAR out of the gravel parking area and headed in the direction of Dawning Cottage, but did not turn in at the roadside sign. The public road continued for a short distance and then curved northward, following the coastline. Laurie had driven this road to the standing stones, so she knew there was no village near nor tavern, nothing but scattered farms on the summer-green moors.

Eric pulled his car to a stop just beyond the bend of the road, within a quarter mile of Dawning, and switched off the engine. Now there were only sounds of a lonely island. Rain beat hard upon the roof and windshield. Restless ocean waves crashed against the rocks at the base of the cliffs. A foghorn wailed mournfully through the gray-white brume.

The windows fogged over. "Our room with a view?" she asked. "This is your private place?"

"Where is your faith? We can't talk in this cramped space, with the rain pounding like a hundred drums over our heads. It's near. Only a short walk."

"A walk? Why not? It's a fine afternoon for a walk."

He got out and came around to open the door for her. His hair blowing and the rain pelting his face, he offered his hand. Laurie, ducking under her rain hood, stepped out into thick, wet grass.

"Why am I going along with this?" she asked.

"Because you're curious. And you've a sense of adventure, just as I have. And you like the idea of being alone with me."

He was squeezing her hand tightly, leading her into curtains of fog. "It might be a little slippery on the cliff, but I'll hang on to you."

Laurie balked. "We're going down the cliff in this weather? Are you mad? For what? A leisure stroll on the beach?"

"Oh, trust me. In a few moments we'll be cozy and dry. Hold tightly to me as we descend. The grass will be slippery."

A gust of wind kicked off the ocean. Laurie held her hood in place with one hand, while the other remained in Eric's warm grasp. There was no path leading down the rocky precipice. Not far below the crown of the cliff a cave entrance appeared as a black slab of darkness. Eric ducked inside, drawing her in beside him. The cliff seemed to swallow them.

The noise of rain abruptly ended. They stood in dry, gray silence. Light filtered in softly through the entrance. Wisps of thick fog floated upon the light like hovering ghosts.

Laurie's exclamation resounded from the walls of rock. "This cave is all but hidden, Eric! How did you ever find it?"

"Quite by accident, when I was exploring the area."

"A secret cave! Oh, how tongues would wag."

"More so if we tried to find privacy under the roof of Dawning Cottage. But we can forget the rest of the world here. It's the perfect lair for medieval dragons, don't you think? But I've walked about and found no dragon, so why not take off your wet coat and get comfortable? I've left some candles for light, if I can find them."

He began to search an inner archway while he dug into the pockets of his raincoat and produced a book of matches and a small cassette tape player.

He found the candles. In a moment the cave filled with weak, flickering light as the wicks caught and held the flames. Eric said, "We should have brought a bottle of wine."

The walls kept out the cold sea wind and blowing rain. Laurie shook the rain from her coat and sat down on the floor in the eerie, dancing light. "Are you absolutely sure this cave isn't inhabited by a dragon?"

"Should it turn out to be, my lady, consider the beast as well as slain."

"Slain by a Gypsy in pink."

Eric glanced down. "Oh, you mean my winner's shirt? I wore it because I knew there would be card games at the tavern on an inclement day like this."

"A lucky shirt? You mean you're superstitious? You?"

"Luck has nothing to do with it, nor superstition. The color pink has the power to tranquilize, so my opponents are calmer and therefore slower to react."

Laurie studied the man who was seated beside her in the candlelight. "Are you serious? I've read research studies on color... how violent criminals are calmed by prison cells painted pink. But Eric, a shirt?"

He grinned. "When players sit opposite this bright pink, it commands their focus quite subconsciously. It makes a difference, sometimes a great difference, in how they play."

"You sound like an expert on influencing people's subconscious minds."

He shot her a look that she could not interpret.

"Is it true?" she asked.

"I suppose so."

"You don't really gamble, do you? You play only to win."

Eric cleared his throat. "It's simple strategy. The player who is best at reading body language and influencing subconscious thought wins."

"And since you view life itself as a game, your strategy applies to everything. Is life a serious game, Eric?"

"I don't think so."

"Most people think so."

"That's what makes them vulnerable."

She sensed Eric was ill at ease with this conversation, perhaps because he knew his so-called "strategy" straddled the fence between honesty and cheating. Honesty—surely the richest of all legacies—had not been Eric's inheritance. From his father he'd learned more devious skills on how to influence people than Laurie ever wanted to know about.

She reached for his pocket-size recorder and switched on the tape. The music sang out into the dark corners and echoed from the cavern walls.

"That music . . ." Laurie mused, feeling the now familiar spell of it sweep over her. "Do you carry it with you all the time, or did you anticipate our being out here alone?"

"I dared to hope the two of us might find ourselves together."

"Dared hope, nothing. You insinuate and estimate all my feelings. You see me as a . . . a player in a game."

"Forgive me," he said softly.

She withdrew into silence. Candlelight on Eric's face made him appear more handsome than she had ever seen him. The pink shirt, exposing a portion of his tanned chest and his muscular arms, was impossible to look away from. His eyes were so pale in the ghostly light that she could see no depth to them. When the pale eyes looked directly into hers, they seemed to transfer some secret power to her. She felt the power surge.

"Eric . . . are you absolutely sure you are real?"

"As real as you want me to be."

"Then perhaps I want you to be a fantasy, since it's my move in this specific game. After all, I *am* a player. Aren't I?"

"You are." He reached out to touch her face. "But I don't know how to be a fantasy when the blood is running so hot in my veins. I'm not used to the heat inside me, Laurie. My blood pulses hot because of *my* fantasy. You are my fantasy. I never thought fate would bring me anywhere near a woman like you—with your beauty and your honesty and your gentle heart."

Her fingers trembled over his. She stroked his hand, exploring the shape of each finger, the rise of each vein and the curve of each knuckle. Powerful hands. They had held weapons, no doubt of it. And they had known the touch of women—but perhaps never the touch of a woman he deeply loved. Could that be? She lifted his hand to her lips.

His hand drew softly, slowly away, to be replaced by his lips. He kissed her deeply.

The kiss spun round and round in her head and body, as if she were being spun into an intricate spiderweb. Tender and strong—his kiss. Tender and strong—the finespun web of his power numbed her resistance and left her trembling.

Her emotions were out of her control. Laurie weakly pulled away from his embrace and took a gulp of the sleepy, musky air of the dragon's lair.

"Damn, Eric, I'm mesmerized! You . . . this hidden cave . . . that music . . . and the worst is, I don't even want you to be explainable!"

His fingertips were moving slowly over her throat, down to her breasts. "I wonder if you've any inkling of the power of your own spell, my love. You've laid waste my every resolve to keep us at arm's length."

"What a horrid resolve!"

"I know that now. I didn't know at first."

She closed her eyes and luxuriated in his touch.

"Eric, this cave is probably the most private place on the island, which makes it the most dangerous for us, and you knew that. It doesn't say much for your resolve."

"It speaks for my wanting you, Laurie. My desire for you is taking over my every thought." His hand, moving gently on her breast, ceased its caresses but remained pressed against her. "Sometimes it's confusing being human."

"I like you when you're . . . human."

"That's good, because I'm getting more human by the second. Touching you is the same as remembering desires I'd forgotten I had. . . ."

He gently pushed her sweater from her shoulders and slid the buttons of her silk blouse through their buttonholes. Laurie moved against the caresses of his hands, closing her eyes, memorizing the features of his face with her fingertips until he bent to her and kissed her more deeply than before, open-mouthed, now savagely hungry.

The need that swept over her was beyond anything she had known existed. His heart pounded against hers, their heartbeats found each other and began to beat together.

His hand brushed aside nylon and lace to explore as he kissed her.

"Eric . . . I'm melting. . . ."

"I can feel you melting," he whispered. "But don't worry. You're safe with me."

"How can you say that?"

"I mean, I'll be...kind to you...gentle with you. Don't be afraid of me."

"Eric..."

"Let me love you...." he whispered. Then his lips against hers smothered their words.

Deep within her a small voice screamed, *This shouldn't be happening!* But the small voice had no force against the louder sound of Eric's pulse, pumping blood from his heart through his body...to the loins that pressed against her in the heat of needing her.

Wriggling with new discomfort in his tight jeans, he unfastened them and urged her hand toward him. But feeling her trembling, he stopped and squeezed her hand reassuringly.

"What's wrong?" he asked gently. "Isn't it okay? You are protected, aren't you?"

"It's just that...it's that I barely know you, Eric. I'm still curious about you. I'm in awe all over again each time I look at you...at your face that's so unfairly handsome...at your body...the way you move.... As long as I'm in awe of you, you'll be a stranger."

He kissed the hand he was holding. "I understand. God knows how I stand in awe of *you*, Laurie. But being a man, with the reckless passion of a man, I tend to be impatient, rushing in, rushing you. That won't do." He smiled gently. "Don't be in awe of me. Just...get to know me."

With this he leaned over and removed his shoes and socks. He rose, stripped off his clothes and stood naked, silhouetted in the misty light of the cave entrance.

Laurie felt the flush of heat on her cheeks. "Thanks for proving to me you aren't rushed."

He laughed. "No, I'm not. I'm giving you a chance to get used to me. To all of me."

She could only stare at him. "I don't believe you. Your body is . . . you know perfectly well how beautiful you are. Are you reading my thoughts as I look at you?"

"I'm trying to put you at ease. Isn't it working?"

She laughed. "Tell me—if I took off all my clothes, would it put you at ease?"

"Uh . . . no."

"I didn't think so."

"That's different," he argued. "Isn't it?"

"No."

"I'm only eliminating the aforementioned awe. You are seeing before you just a representative of the standard human male."

"You are mad if you think you are representative of the standard. . . ."

"Well, not counting the standard, then." He grinned. "Thanks to you I've raised the standard."

She cringed. "That's one of the most terrible puns I've ever heard."

"Forgive me. I didn't know you had a shy streak."

Her laughter came, delayed. "I didn't know it, either. You were bragging just now."

"I shouldn't do that, should I?" Eric spread his coat on the cold floor inside out and sat down beside her. "Now," he said. "Where were we?"

"I've completely forgotten."

Reflections of the candle flames created dances of light and shadow on his body.

He reached over and touched her shoulder. "You are shy, Laurie. Didn't anybody ever warn you about Englishmen?"

"I've always heard Englishmen are ultracivilized."

"There. You see?"

"Do I know an Englishman?"

"My whole strategy is for you to get to know one."

"So you claim to both, then? Englishman and Gypsy."

"Mmm. Take your pick." He drew nearer, caressing her arm, leaning close to kiss her.

His kiss immediately brought back the magic, but he seemed closer now, because she could feel the warmth of his body against her. Eric appeared to be as much at ease as if he were clothed, perhaps because his body was perfectly proportioned and tanned by the summer sun.

She threw her arms around him, hugging him close. His heart was beating heavily as it had before. His skin felt warm to her fingers as they moved sensually along his back. The muscles were hard and solid. The feel of him caused the spell of helplessness to float over her once more.

His lips were on hers again; then he was kissing her throat and her shoulder, and she trembled in anticipation.

Pulling her over him, Eric lay down on his back against the coat. Her hair fell forward as he kissed her, and he ran his fingers through it, brushing it back. Her hands began to move in small circles on his chest.

He whispered, "Touch me, Laurie. Touch all of me until I'm not a stranger any more."

Stranger or not, I love you, Laurie thought. It might be a wild and reckless love, like his for her, but it was love nevertheless—stronger than she knew how or wanted to fight. Straightening, she gazed down at him. "Your body..." she muttered.

"My body is yours. To do with what you will. Everything you will."

Her slow caresses were savored dreams, every one. Gifts to him. He lay still, his eyes on her face, his hands sliding sensually over her thighs.

"All of me." He guided her, taking her hand. "I want you to know me...."

At what point the tape stopped playing, Laurie didn't know. The music remained, alive and enchanting, and the music was Eric. His beauty, his passion. His body was an offering for her to love. Everything else faded away—the rain, the echoes of the ocean, all the days and hours she had lived before.

She leaned over him. Kisses followed the path of her caresses—long, exploring, gentle, secret—until his eyes closed and a moan issued from his throat.

The sound awakened her to the vibrations of Eric's need. He too was trembling. His voice, whispering her name, was trembling.

"I'm only human," he whispered. "And helpless with wanting you. You're going to finish me."

Laurie rose to her feet, stripped off her clothes and stood over him, between his legs, looking down at him.

"You're beautiful beyond my wildest dreams," he said.

His eyes burned, so hot with passion that they had lost their paleness. His arms reached up to her.

"Come here to me."

Trembling, her knees shaking, she lowered her body to his. Slowly, luxuriously. Her eyes closed and all the world went away but him. But them. Their bodies synchronized, defining love. Moaning, he grasped her hands tightly. Her name formed silently on his lips.

With a great intake of breath he released the grasp on her hand and began to stroke the sides of her body and her breasts. "Now . . ." he whispered. "We are one."

She bent forward, moving her hips, interpreting and responding to the sensations of their bodies, bonded . . . his hands, touching . . . his eyes, reflecting only the images of love.

He found the musical rhythm of her body. She felt the power of his hands on her hips, guiding, strengthening, building the tempo of their love to a crescendo they could no longer maintain.

Time dissolved into a nocturne of fire. His moan resounded from the dark cavern walls. Laurie's body shook and then went limp over his.

His embrace was more tender than ever before. Eric held her tightly against him, and their hearts drummed hard as if the pounding would never stop.

"My love," he whispered, stroking her hair as she settled down in his arms beside him.

WHEN THE FINAL SMALL FLAME was swallowed by the melted wax of the last burning candle, it disappeared with a tiny poof. The cave was cloaked in darkness.

In silence that did not seem silence, he had held her close for a long time. But when the last candle burned out, the echoes of the cave breathed a loneliness that made her shudder.

"Are you cold?" he asked.

"I don't think so. Your body is warm." She shifted against the lumps of their crumpled clothes. "You've been very quiet, Eric."

"Thinking about you."

"What about me?"

"Are you all right?"

She hesitated, because there was something not quite right in his voice. "Of course. Why wouldn't I be?"

Silence again.

She asked, "Eric, why do I sense a certain regret on your part?"

"Regret? Regret us? How could I?"

"*Something* is bothering you."

"I suppose I was thinking that you're too good for me."

Laurie was listening carefully for hints of what the problem could be. "Why? Because you're full of mischief?"

"Precisely."

"Oh, Eric."

He stirred and kissed her forehead. "Don't get me wrong, Laurie. Making love with you is the sweetest thing I've ever known in my life. My feelings for you are so strong I don't know what to do with them."

It is guilt, she thought with sudden panic. *Why am I sensing guilt now, in Eric, when I never once sensed it in Brian?*

If Eric was suffering guilt, it could only mean that by being with her, he was betraying someone else. Damn. He had never actually said he was free, but after the indignant comments about Brian, surely this couldn't be, unless . . .

She touched his bare shoulder. "I know so little about you, Eric. I don't even know whether you're married."

"Married? Good Lord, what do you take me for?"

"Do you have a special woman in your life?"

"At this moment, yes. She's lying beside me, asking crazy questions."

"You know what I mean. Is there a woman in London who would hate you if she were to walk into this cave right now?"

"Well, love, I don't know. But there's no woman whose sudden appearance here would upset me—except for our lack of privacy. Why would you think so?"

"Something seems to be on your mind, bothering you."

"You are on my mind, nothing else. I swear."

Not altogether convinced, Laurie closed her eyes and breathed in the male fragrance of him, absorbing his touch through her skin—a touch that heated her blood.

She stirred. "The music has stopped. I'll just turn over the tape."

"No," he said.

The abruptness of his reply startled her. "Why not? I thought you loved this music. You called it our music."

"I'm tired of it."

"Eric! Now I know something's wrong!"

He stroked her bare shoulder tenderly. "Nothing's wrong. I'll sing to you instead." He began to hum the melody of an old English folk song. The tune was vaguely familiar. His beautiful deep voice sang it like the incantations of a spell. She closed her eyes, absorbing his very being and knowing she loved him.

When the song was finished, she asked, "Where did you learn it?"

"I can't remember. I seem to have always known it."

"Eric, please let me borrow the little pocket recorder with our music tape. You might be tired of it, but I'm not. I want to listen to that music and think of us...and the Gypsy fires."

"You'll get tired of it, too."

"Please. I won't keep it long."

There was reluctance in the deep sigh that was his only sign of consent. It made no sense to Laurie that he might not want her to borrow the tape, since he had been the one who introduced her to it and had played it constantly for her.

Now the cave was silent. Eric dozed lightly against her shoulder. Laurie listened to his breathing until she herself slid into a shallow sleep.

Soon, out of the darkness, she heard his voice. "The rain has stopped."

Stirring, she brushed at her tangled hair. "How do you know?"

"I can see the sky beyond the entrance." He sat up. "I suppose we ought to go."

Laurie couldn't think of a reason to go. Except perhaps that their candles had burned down and the cave was quite dark. She didn't move.

"The rain will begin again soon," he said. "And going back up the cliffside is going to be much more difficult than coming down."

"If you insist," she said softly.

Eric drew his arms around her and kissed her. "I don't want to leave *you*, my sweet, only this cave."

"This cave is haunted. Isn't it? By your ornery little spirits?"

He laughed. "For us it has been a noble room, a palace room, willingly lent, but they seem to want it returned, since they took the darkness back."

"What is really bothering you, Eric? Something is."

"You already asked that question, and I told you, nothing. You couldn't have made me happier. You made me the luckiest man alive."

He kissed her with a new tenderness that told her what he had just said was true. Whatever was wrong was something else. But whether he was willing to admit it or not, Laurie was certain that it had something to do with their having made love. He had wanted it, enticed her more deliciously than she had ever been enticed. Had even read her mind and known she wanted him. And then he had drawn into some damn secret that *did* in some way have to do with her ... or with his loving her.

THEY RETURNED to the Red Wolf, and Laurie went directly to her car and drove back to Dawning Cottage, in time to shower and change her clothes for tea. Eric was nearly an hour behind her because he tarried at the tavern.

He came in looking rumpled and a little sullen.

"What be ye up to, lad?" Jeanne Gunn asked. "Gambling, I'll wager. And from the looks of ye, ye've had the worst of it."

"Oh, it's the rain. I'm bloody sick of rain. It seeps through the skin until it chills the blood."

"Hot tea will warm ye. And a bit of nourishment."

He thanked her, sat down, and gave Laurie a quick and private smile before sinking into a silence that seemed to come from deep thought. He showed no further interest in entering into conversation with the three women.

Laurie pondered his remark. The rain that had brought them together today. Perhaps, though, it was all he knew to say to explain his less than immaculate appearance.

Marion stared at him with the same look Laurie had observed in the dining room last night—a gaze that combined fascination with contempt . . . and thinly covered adoration.

Eric was distracted, and Laurie didn't think it was by Marion. He stayed only a short time in the fire-warmed parlor, then excused himself. He'd barely nibbled at the sweets on the tea tray. Was he—as he had told her today—a man in love?

They heard his heavy step on the stairs and in his bedroom just overhead.

Marion smoothed her dark skirt and primly picked up her teacup. "You've been out all day in the rain, Laurie. Surely not to the standing stones."

"I went to the Red Wolf for an ale or two."

"I say, really!"

Amused, Laurie thought, *How indignant this woman is for someone who claims to be more worldly than a marine on shore leave.* She began, "Maybe you'd enjoy—"

From the floor above came a crash so loud that Laurie stopped in midsentence, and Marion's tea went flying when she jumped. The bang was followed by a piercing jangle of shattered glass falling to the floor.

Mrs. Gunn was on her feet at once. "What on earth?"

Marion began to shriek while already dabbing at the spilled tea. "It's Eric! He must have fallen through the window!"

7

ERIC HAD GONE UPSTAIRS so tightly coiled with frustration that he knew the spring was about to snap. With nothing and no one upon which to vent his anger—except himself—he had stormed about his room, regretting he had gone in for tea at all. Mrs. Gunn's cake settled like a stone in his stomach, and Marion Huckles had looked at him like a hound crouched in wait for an unwary hare. Twice yesterday Marion had heard part of the subliminal love tape and absorbed its hidden messages, and her entire body language had begun to change when he'd walked into the room. Damn.

The effect of the tapes was unbelievably fast and unbelievably strong. Laurie MacDonald had become as enchanted as if she were under the spells of the ancients—hell, this spell was stronger than anything the ancients had ever come up with. This was subconscious programming. She was subconsciously programmed to fall in love with him.

He had led her on, lured her to the cave, turned on his charms. And knowingly, deliberately, taken advantage of this unfair meddling into her subconscious thoughts.

There were names for men like him. He'd been called a few of them, but had never thought he'd hear the curses raise a howl from his own brain.

Laurie had trusted him.

Damn!

Heated by his anger, Eric pulled off his sweater and paced, thinking of her trusting eyes. So wildly infatuated was he by this woman, he'd been unable to resist her. He'd tossed away every principle he'd ever lived by... surrendered the last shred of self-discipline he'd owned... given in to his lust and called it love.

The spider had been caught in his own web!

He came to a halt in front of the mirror over the washstand and gazed at his reflection, watching his own eyes silver with anger at what he saw. With a teeth-grinding grunt his anger flew out of control, and his fist slammed into the mirror with a savage blow. The reflection of the face he was determined to destroy cracked into a thousand shards and fell, crashing onto the polished wooden floor.

Eric swore a violent oath. The crash and blood on his hand had startled him into the realization of what he had just done. Already he could hear Mrs. Gunn's quick footsteps in the downstairs hall. She was shouting his name frantically.

To stop blood from dripping onto the carpet, he pulled his white T-shirt over his head and wrapped his hand. Stepping over the pile of glass, he opened the door and called down, "That was your mirror breaking! A stupid accident. Sorry. I'll replace it straight-away."

"Are you hurt?" She was puffing up the stairs.

"No." He examined his hand—two shallow cuts. He'd been lucky; the bleeding was minimal. He moved out onto the landing. "If you'll show me where your brush and dustpan are, I'll get the glass cleaned up."

"By all the dead saints, Eric, how could you break a mirror?"

"I looked in it and it just cracked all to hell."

"Come on, lad. Give me a run, at least."

"Oh, don't look at me like that," he said. "It was an accident."

"Well now, I'd hardly suppose it'd be a deliberate act of will." Jeanne Gunn raised both arms in the air. "Never mind. You're alive to tell about it, that's all I care. The broom is in the back cupboard, off the kitchen."

"I'll have a mirror sent out from London," he called as he descended the stairs two steps at a time, his shirt still binding his right hand.

To his dismay, Laurie and Marion were standing in the hall, watching him with curiosity. He couldn't meet the eyes of either woman.

"What in the name of sanity happened?" Marion pressed with obstinacy. "One would have thought a duel to the death was being fought up there!"

"Quite right, it was. There's one pest of a gnat who will never see the light of day again."

"A gnat? Eric, you lie! It sounded as though the entire building was being demolished around us, and you blame it on a gnat?"

"The little pest asked for it," Eric said mildly while he turned and headed for the kitchen. "Don't fret so much, Marion. I've left most of the building still standing."

"Right good of you!" she called after him.

Laurie had said nothing at all about the mysterious crash. Only her eyes were questioning, and he had avoided them as much as he could. Guilt was an unfamiliar emotion for Eric Sinclair. It had begun to sting hard while they were still in the cave and Laurie was lying next to him, warm and beautiful and filled with love for him. Laurie had noticed something wrong, though. She was one of the few people who had ever seen through him when he didn't want his emotions read. What could she see now? he wondered, when he came down the stairway with no plausible explanation for a mirror bashed in an anger tantrum?

Seven years of bad luck, he thought. Starting now.

When Eric returned from the back pantry, carrying the brush and dustpan, both Marion and Laurie had gone back into the warmth of the parlor, and Mrs. Gunn was upstairs surveying damage.

Some thirty minutes later, coming down with a dustpan full of glass shards, Eric began to sense trouble. His ears had picked up the music before he was fully aware of what was wrong, but as he passed by the closed parlor door, he heard it clearly. Laurie was playing that damned tape in the parlor!

When he'd reluctantly lent it to her because he could find no excuse not to, it had never occurred to him that Laurie would play that music anywhere but in the privacy of her room upstairs. Even that, under the disastrous circumstances of the afternoon, was bad enough. Eric felt a shudder form at the base of his spine. *If Marion was in there . . .*

He pushed open the door with the caution of a hunter trying to avoid his own snare and peered inside.

Laurie and Marion were seated near the fireplace. Half-empty teacups were on the table. Each had a book in her lap—Marion the notebook that had almost become an appendage, and Laurie a thick book with a black and red cover. But reading had been abandoned while they sat, heads back, eyes closed, listening to a tape with subliminal messages recorded every few seconds. One suggestion over and over, at least a hundred times. Len's voice under the music on the same frequency. Eric didn't even know what the words were, except that they could convince the listener she was crazily in love. *Could and did.*

He was filled with panic.

Gasping on a great intake of breath, he entered the room, unseen by either of the women who sat lost in the strains of the dangerous Gypsy music.

He placed himself squarely in the center of the room and shouted, "Has anybody seen the aspirin?"

Marion jumped so violently, her notebook pitched to the floor, spewing out papers all around her feet.

Laurie's eyes flew open. She stared up at Eric, disoriented, as if he were a fantasy who lived inside the music and had no business being a living, breathing, shouting man. He saw himself in the shine of her eyes as he stood in the white glare of the lamp, a glare he knew illuminated his scar. Laurie's eyes fixed on the scar, and in those seconds Eric, reading her eyes, could as easily read her mind. Since the cave this afternoon he was her secret lover. In the aura of guitar and zither and violin rainbows she had been remembering their love.

"What's the matter?" Laurie asked finally.

"I can't find the aspirin! I stole it from you and now it's gone!"

"Where would you have put it?"

"If I knew that, it wouldn't be gone."

To his relief Laurie reached over and switched off the music, remembering, perhaps, that he had said he was tired of it. Or perhaps she thought it no longer matched the atmosphere.

In the new, dull silence Marion began to rise out of her reverie. Her eyes bore into him like little glowing pieces of charcoal. "That's the second time tonight you have frightened me out of my skin! Are you having fun? Eric, why are you looking like that . . . and just standing there, pawing the ground like a stallion?"

He was learning a new meaning for the word "backfire," for the subliminal commands were affecting Marion in a less than gentle way. This might be what he deserved, Eric thought, but Marion didn't deserve it, and neither did Laurie.

"Who has the aspirin?" he growled. By this time he really wanted to know.

"Who turned off the music?" Marion demanded. "Laurie, don't turn off the music! I adore that music. Eric, you *must* hear this, you *must*! If you would sit and relax and listen to this wonderful music, you wouldn't need an aspirin."

"He's heard it," Laurie said. "It's Eric's tape." She rose, setting her book upon the table. "Let's try to retrace your steps, then, or else find Jeanne and see if she knows where the aspirin bottle is. What hurts? Your head?"

He could with honesty have answered that his hand was throbbing badly from attacking the nifty cad who had stared back at him from the mirror on his bedroom wall. But if he mentioned his hand, she would naturally ask how he had hurt it. He merely nodded in the affirmative, because his head was beginning to throb, too.

"Eric's tape!" Marion exclaimed. "Had I known you were a man who likes this sort of marvelous music, I'd have been a bit more . . ."

His eyebrows rose, and his voice deepened to a groan. "More what?"

"More . . . tolerant of your eccentricities."

"I have no eccentricities."

"All right. We shan't use that label. We'll say character highlights instead. Yes, a far better phrase. I'd have been more attuned to your highlights."

"I hope highlights can be cured with aspirin," he said, rubbing his aching hand.

Laurie was searching the lower shelves in the parlor. "The last time I saw that bottle, it was in this room the night of your serious injury. When you stole it, did you take it upstairs?"

"I don't know."

Marion began to circle about him like a bird of prey. "Where does it hurt?" she asked.

"I just remembered, I left the aspirin upstairs," he said. Eric turned to leave, but his path to the door was blocked by Marion in a posture he had never before seen on a human being. Her shoulders were back, her head raised slightly, and her right arm bent at the elbow, extended forward with the palm turned up. She looked like a statue, except that no water was spouting from her palm.

He cringed. The exposed wrist was one of the most telling signs of sexual interest. Laurie had quite unconsciously exposed her wrists to him in the Red Wolf. Laurie had also looked at him, her pupils dilated, just as Marion's were now. These were the sure signals of sexual desire that he'd been looking for. Of course, it was easier to call it mind reading. When he picked up subconscious giveaways, people resented the truth less when he called it mind reading. With Laurie it had been a victory, but now he was getting the same signals from Marion.

This he hadn't bargained for. He stared at the blue veins of her wrist, trying to determine his next move. It wouldn't do to embarrass her; it wasn't her fault she found him irresistible. He simply blinked and took a step around her toward the door.

Behind him Laurie asked, "Is there anything I can do for you?"

"Yes," he said. "Give me back the tape."

"No!" Marion protested.

"Why?" Laurie asked softly.

"Because the painkiller by itself won't help. If I don't have my...music, I can't relax. Please tell Jeanne I won't be down for dinner."

Laurie handed him the little recorder. "You're acting strangely, Eric. You seemed energetic enough...earlier."

"It's nothing," he lied. "I'll talk to you later, all right?"

She nodded and watched him reach around Marion's stiff form, open the parlor door, and dive into the cold hallway, gripping the little tape player tightly.

He left silence in his wake.

Marion restrained a gasp. She looked at Laurie, then stared at her fingernails with forced calm. "Good heavens," she said, knowing Eric could hear her. "Can you imagine a grown man getting so upset over a gnat?"

Normally, overhearing such a remark would have brought on a hefty laugh, but not this time. Upstairs, he tossed the machine aside and sat down on his bed, leaning his head into his hands, rubbing his temples.

The world moves by manipulation, he thought. *There are the manipulators and those who are their prey. A man who understands this, by his nature imposes his will on others. He must, because he cannot think of himself as a victim of the world's other suggestion-makers.*

Laurie was his prey, then. And so was Marion—one by intention, the other as a result of his own bungling. Eric wasn't used to making errors of this magnitude. The whole damn project was a mistake.

Some of it was Laurie's fault. He had come to want her and to love her, perhaps in that order, perhaps not. He had fallen so hard for her, everything else around him had run amok. Laurie had spun a web within a web.

And caught him in it.

THAT NIGHT he opened the door of her room just a crack and whispered her name.

"Laurie? I couldn't knock because knocking is too loud. I saw the light under your door. What are you doing?"

"Reading." She motioned him in.

He left the door slightly ajar. "Thinking about me?"

"Yes."

She was propped in the chair with a quilt thrown over her shoulders. The lamplight shone on her soft hair and glinted on the thin gold chain she wore around her neck over her dark sweater. Her hair was tied back with a wide, pink ribbon.

He sat down on the bed opposite her. "I can't get you out of my mind. This afternoon when we were together...I've never known such moments, never in my life. Your love is like a drug that will be in my bloodstream forever. I saw your eyes downstairs when you had been listening to the music. Your eyes haunt me, Laurie. They always will."

"Haunt." She closed her book slowly. "Your word *haunt* has uncomfortable meanings. It implies something already past or something to do with loss or guilt. What's in my eyes that you don't want to see?"

"I didn't mean it like that."

"I think you did."

"All I want to see in your eyes is the reflection of me. That's what I saw today... in the cave ... in the parlor. And now. I see me in your eyes."

She gazed at him. "I see you cut your hand on the mirror."

He opened his palm. "It's nothing. I'm accident-prone, as you know. I always carry a supply of plasters with me."

"Is your head all right?"

"My head?"

"Your headache. Knowing what a healthy appetite you have, I thought only pain would cause you to miss dinner."

"I wasn't in the mood for dinner conversation. I talked Jeanne Gunn into allowing me to make a sandwich when no one was looking, and took it to my room with a glass of milk. Now that everybody else is asleep, I came to invite you for a drink."

"A drink? Nothing more?"

"Perhaps something more."

She pulled the blanket from her shoulders. "You think I can't resist you, don't you?"

"I know you can't."

"I see. Reading my mind again."

He offered his hand. She let him lead her to his room. Inside, a fire burned in the little fireplace and the large room was peaceful with a sleepy warmth. Shadows of the fire whispered on the walls and soft music played.

"What is this music?" she asked. "It isn't *our* music that you said you were sick of, but wanted to listen to anyway when you asked for your tape back." Eric was prone to mood swings, she thought.

"Who cares what it is?" he asked mildly. "I brought back a bottle of fine sherry from the Red Wolf."

The bottle was already open. He poured out two small portions and handed her a glass.

"I can't stop thinking about how beautiful you are and how beautiful today was. I'm a man obsessed."

"I haven't thought of anything else, either."

Eric set down his glass. His hand brushed through her hair, stroking softly. The back of her neck tingled and a shiver moved through her.

"Are you cold?"

"No. It's you making me tremble."

He wrapped his arms around her. "I know so little about you. Tell me what your life is like."

She wrinkled her nose to show impatience with the subject at this time of night, in the arms of the man she loved. "We already know you and I have nothing whatsoever in common, Eric. I'm the product of a small Ohio town—Miss Average. After high school I attended the local junior college and then the state university, where I got hooked on mythology of the Middle Ages, along with physical anthropology, my main field of study. I spent a year in Greece after I graduated, and then went back to Ohio and took a position in a state-operated lab, working on various assignments, usually having to do with identifying and reconstructing bones. There, you see, except for that year in Greece, I've lived in Ohio all my life."

"You forgot the part about Brian," he reminded her.

"Brian is already forgotten."

"So soon? How can you forget a lover so soon?"

"When one is betrayed," she said. "When one is lied to deliberately and with calculation, the humiliation and anger are more effective than any drug to deaden the feelings and the memory."

She felt Eric tense.

"Don't feel guilty," she said.

"What?"

"For telling me about Brian. We've been through that. I'm grateful to you for it, and anyway, if Brian's deceitful game hadn't caught up with him at Loch Ness, I wouldn't be here with you."

"I'm sorry I brought up the past," he said.

"Why?" She moved her fingers up and down his arm. "Eric, you have a rather devious nature, you know. Do *you* lie to your lovers?"

"I've never lied about my marital status."

"That isn't what I mean. You have been married, haven't you? How long were you married?"

"A month less than two years."

"Divorce?"

"She died of a rare blood disease."

"How awful!"

"I knew she was terminally ill when I married her," he said softly. "But our time together was good. Have we finished talking about the past? I'd rather talk about the present."

"Eric . . ." she began. This last revelation about him confused her. Somehow it didn't fit her image of him, and she wanted to know more about his tragic marriage in order to better understand the man. But this wasn't the time. Some other day she would bring it up again.

"Or better," he was saying, "we could talk about nothing at all." He lifted her glass from her hand, set it on the table beside his and urged her playfully onto the bed.

"I'll say it again, Laurie. My mind is too crowded with thoughts of you to think about anything else. I even went out and walked around in what's left of the rain."

"A bout of pneumonia would give you something to think about."

"I never catch anything from exposure to the elements."

"Please don't say rain is your element."

He laughed. "I could be rain—a gentle rain that caresses your body." His fingertips caressed her. He kissed her lightly. "Or I could be sunshine warming your lovely shoulders..."

Eyes closed, feeling his fluttery kisses on her face and neck, Laurie fell helplessly under his spell. Wanting him more than she had known she could want a man, she was frightened of... and in awe of... her own emotions. Something wild existed in her love for Eric, some devil-may-care recklessness that had no connection with the rest of her life. Yet at the same time, from deep within, a warning had been flashing like a beacon of light. It was like advertising beacons she had seen from time to time—those that move across the sky, coming from a source one can't find. This one originated inside herself and it beamed toward whatever thing it was that Eric was hiding from her.

When he kissed her the warnings dimmed, for his kisses were filled with love. Love radiated from his strong hands when he touched her. Her fear of him was only the residue of relationships with others who had hurt her, she told herself. Eric was not Brian. Eric was not any other man...."

"Laurie," he said. "Do you believe me when I say I love you?"

"Yes." And because she felt that danger signal again, she asked, "Is there some reason I shouldn't?"

He shook his head. "It's important you believe me. I didn't plan this... didn't plan to love you."

"It's not the sort of thing one plans."

"I know. But the point is, all other plans are abolished. I'm . . . we're going from here . . . as if we had just . . . just met normally like . . . people do. . . ."

As his arms tightened around her, Laurie observed, "You're stammering. What are you talking about? You're not making a great lot of sense."

"Men in love don't have to make sense, I suppose. I tried to fight loving you, and I can't. So I won't."

"I think I tried to fight loving you, too, but it was a lost cause from the very start."

"Just love me, then," he said.

He pulled her tighter into his embrace and kissed her with more passion than ever before, telling her with the kiss that she belonged to him and only to him.

She rolled up on top of him on the bed. Her lips trembled over his forehead, cheeks and chin, where her tongue outlined the pattern of his scar. He moaned when she kissed his neck, then his ear, following the trail of kisses with her tongue, exploring. It was her way of possessing him, too.

Licking playfully at his earlobe, Laurie paused when she felt a tiny bump.

"What is it?" he asked.

"This mark on your earlobe! Do you have pierced ears?"

"One. Since my childhood. My father's idea. He thought a gold earring gave me an authentic, Gypsy look."

"But why? I thought he didn't want you to be a Gypsy."

"There were times when it was useful to him for me to be a homeless waif. It came in handy when a part of his game plan—his con game—was convincing people the two of us were strangers, so we could work together without drawing suspicion."

"He actually did such things? Eric, that's shocking!"

"It was a way of life. I survived."

"Aren't you bitter?"

"I don't know. I never sorted out my feelings about it." He touched her face lovingly. "Come on, sweet, we have better things to think about tonight."

"Has it grown shut?"

"What?"

"The hole in your ear."

"I have no idea. I forgot about it years ago."

She snuggled against him. "Your life has been very unusual."

"Does my questionable identity bother you?"

"No, but your secret does."

The rhythm of his breathing changed. "What do you mean?"

"I'm not without certain powers of insight myself, and I feel you have some secret."

His hand was now caressing her bare back under her sweater. "You don't fully trust me. I've always realized that. I've never proved you could trust me. Trust is an earned thing."

Her voice was becoming weaker under his mesmerizing touch. "Trust should be inherent, natural. I don't see trust as something that has to be earned."

"For a fellow like me, it does."

He bent to kiss her again, to end a conversation he hated.

His fingers were moving over the soft swell of her breasts. Anticipation of his love was dulling her senses, making her giddy and wild. She sank into the enchantment of his kiss, submerging deeper and deeper into the bewitchment that was Eric's mysterious kind of love.

She felt her sweater lifted away, felt the warmth of his hands and lips on her breasts. Felt the warmth of his body pressed to hers.

Warmth. This time, not having to protect her from the cold and damp, Eric could allow himself the luxury of exploring her body, as she had explored his. All her hesitation was gone; only desire remained in her eyes, and in the hands that touched his hair and chest and worked at the buttons of his shirt.

He threw off the shirt and drew her close, enjoying the sensation of skin on skin while he kissed her. With a single heave of his body he rolled them both over so that she was on her back, then sprawled above her, smiling down at her, his hair curled over his forehead, broad shoulders shadowing her from the single lamp that burned on the opposite side of the room.

Within seconds his gentle hands had stripped away the rest of her clothes and his own.

She smiled up dreamily. "How did you do that? Your hands are trained in magic."

"You are the magic," he murmured. "You cause my head to swim and my loins to throb with the aching. If I couldn't have you tonight I would go mad."

She closed her eyes and allowed his touch to sweep her into the mystic night. The private night that be-

TAKE 4 MEDICAL ROMANCES FREE

Mills & Boon Medical Romances capture the excitement, intrigue and emotion of a busy medical world. A world often interrupted by love and romance...

We will send you 4 Brand New Medical Romances absolutely Free plus 2 Glass Oyster Dishes and a surprise mystery gift, as your introduction to this superb series.

At the same time we'll reserve a subscription for you to our Reader Service. Every month you could receive the latest four Medical Romances delivered direct to your door Post and Packing Free, plus a free Newsletter packed with competitions, author news and much, much more.

What's more there's no obligation, you can cancel or suspend your subscription at any time. So you've nothing to lose and a whole world of romance to gain!

FREE GIFT

Return this card now and we'll also send you this beautiful set of two Glass Oyster Dishes absolutely FREE.

Fill in the Free Books Coupon overleaf ▼▼

Free Books Certificate

Yes! Please send me my 4 Free Medical Romances, together with my Free Glass Dishes and Mystery gift. Please also reserve a special Reader Service subscription for me. If I decide to subscribe, I shall receive 4 superb new books every month for just £5.80, post and packing free. If I decide not to subscribe, I shall write to you within 10 days. The free books and gifts will be mine to keep in any case.

I understand that I am under no obligation whatsoever - I can cancel or suspend my subscription at any time simply by writing to you.

I am over 18 years of age.

Extra Bonus

We all love surprises, so as well as the Free books and Glass Dishes here's an intriguing mystery gift especially for you. No clues - send off today!

3A1D

Mrs/Miss/Ms _____
(BLOCK CAPITALS PLEASE)

Address _____

_____

_____ Postcode _____

Signature _____

NO STAMP
NEEDED

Reader Service
FREEPOST
PO Box 236
Croydon
Surrey
CR9 9EL

Send No Money Now

longed only to them. His kisses fell over her body like warm raindrops. His hands possessed her. Laurie yielded. There was nothing else she could do.

Eric's love was new. Different. He came from the earth, worshiped the earth and its wild, free spirit, and while he made love to her, she experienced a strange, mysterious bonding, both to the earth and to him—primitive, uninhibited, and utterly real.

"You are not like other men. . . ." she whispered.

"I hope not," he whispered back.

She wondered if he had any idea what she meant. It was entirely possible that he did.

In response to his silent urgings—silent gifts—his moist breath and the intimate gliding of his tongue, Laurie gave her body to him. Sinking as she would sink into the depths of the ocean, she let go and floated on the spinning air of earth.

To belong to this man was to be free. Why, she didn't know or understand in the untamed frenzy of loving him. Laurie only knew that somehow, in some way, the more he took of her, the more he gave. And the ultimate gift was the freedom to love. . . .

Out of control, she moaned and shuddered and trembled. Eric gently moved up over her and pressed slowly, deeply into her. Her tight, hard grasp on his shoulders drew blood; he felt nothing but exhilaration in the willing, possessive seizure of his body.

"And for me . . ." he gasped. "I want you too much . . . too much and in a thousand ways. . . ."

His pulse found the beat of hers, his body rushed its heat into hers, and at the sweet, excruciating moment of release, a joy deep within his soul merged with hers.

8

LAURIE LAY WIDE-AWAKE, staring into the shadows. Eric breathed in the slow, even rhythm of deep sleep. How long she had lain there beside him, she couldn't determine, but the fire had burned down and the room was colder. His body warmed hers. She didn't want to leave him.

But staying was too risky. Marion was on the alert. In fact, the way Marion had been acting around Eric that afternoon, she'd probably be watching closely. Laurie knew she couldn't emerge from Eric's room in the morning. The consequences were simply not worth the risk; it would be impossibly awkward for everybody.

As quietly as possible, Laurie slid out of the bed. Eric, lying on his side, one arm curled above his head, didn't stir. Drawing the blanket over his shoulder, she thought, *He is beautiful in sleep.* It would be easy just to stand beside his bed and watch him sleep until dawn lighted the eastern sky. Her mysterious Gypsy lover, who gave more of himself in lovemaking than any man she'd ever known . . . who rendered her helpless under the seductive abandon he so freely called love.

Tomorrow there would not be rain. Eric had said so. That meant she could drive to the standing stones in the morning. There was a small inn a mile or so from the meadow of the stones, a lovely place for lunch. Private. If Eric joined her there, she could count the hours until she saw him. The chances of him showing up for breakfast were slim.

She decided to write a note, asking him to meet her at the inn for lunch, and leave it beside the bed where he would see it when he woke. The mirror would have been the obvious place, but the mirror, for a reason he hadn't adequately explained, was not there anymore.

The small lamp still burned. As quietly as possible, Laurie began a haphazard search for a paper and pen among the notebooks and electronic equipment on Eric's desk.

A loose-leaf notebook had been pushed under some books. It would surely have a blank page of paper. Gingerly she pulled it out. On the front of the notebook was written Tape #29 S.M. Case File #1. Notes. Inside she found Eric's handwritten jottings, written in the format of a daily log. A glance told her it wasn't a diary, because each page contained several series of number combinations and what appeared to be improvised codes.

One particular word resurfaced over and over.

Curious, Laurie began to read through the entries. A hideous feeling of sinking took form somewhere in her chest, slammed against her stomach and dropped through her body until no sensation but utter weakness remained. Silent words formed on her lips.

My God! she shrieked silently. *What is this?*

The recurring word was *subject*.

Day 1, afternoon. Time of exposure: 21 minutes. Subject exhibited first rudimentary reflexes after approx. 14 minutes. Eye contact, interest in Control.

Day 1, evening. Time of exposure: 47 min. Subject's mood receptive. Cordiality high, excessive eye contact.

Rushing through the log, Laurie's eyes fell on such phrases as "Subject showing high susceptibility." "Subject in excitable state." "Subject's interest in Control correlates directly with time of exposure."

What the hell did this mean?

Tape #29 S.M. The notebook cover read *Tape #29 S.M.* That was the number written on the white, gummed label of Eric's tape—the one she had borrowed from him. She had thought it odd his tape was labeled by numbers and letters rather than the title of the music.

Slowly it began to dawn on her that "exposure" meant time of exposure to the music. "Contact" referred to Eric himself. And "Subject" meant her!

No! It couldn't be!

Eyes brimming with tears, she glanced over at the man who slept soundly in the bed, at peace after their lovemaking. So handsome that his looks startled her every time she saw him. So innocent in sleep.

Laurie grasped hard and desperately for denial. There had to be some mistake, some other explanation for what she was reading! Trembling and with her head growing light, she read further. Direct references to the music began to appear in the entries. Her actions of the past three days were documented. "Occupation with empty tumbler—fondling a cylinder," he had written.

"Eye movement, glances to the right, indicate subconscious resistance to passion." "Suggestion color pink indicator included in tape. Subject responding by wearing pink, shows indicator is effective control."

He described the dilation of her eyes, her posture, the positioning of her hands—signs that had indicated her attraction to him. Because of her exposure to that tape! That damned tape was filled with subliminal messages about sexual attraction! It was a weapon! A subliminal weapon!

Humiliation beyond anything she'd ever experienced fell over Laurie like a suffocating cape.

Fury began to consume her.

"Mind reading, Eric?" she mouthed through clenched teeth, glancing again at the sleeping man.

Rummaging silently and carefully through some of the other papers on his desk produced proof in the form of a brochure. It listed at least two dozen types of "subliminal message tapes," including one numbered #29 S.M., S.M. being the code for subliminal message. "Make her fall in love with you through subliminal commands," the caption advertising this particular tape read. "She will think she is hearing only music. Available in Easy Listening, Pop Music and Classical."

Brightly decorated, Eric's name appeared on the cover, directly under the name Aquarius Recording Company. He not only played these damned tapes, he *manufactured* them! And used her as an experiment to determine how effective the tapes were.

He had used the tapes to seduce her!

Laurie's first impulse was to leap upon him like a screaming banshee of the night and scratch out his eyes.

But who could predict what so powerful a man might do if he were awakened from sleep by a violent, physical assault? Furthermore, what satisfaction would she get out of it? He would just grow angry and use his strength to dump her upon the floor with ease.

Shaking uncontrollably with humiliation and fury, Laurie closed her eyes and tried desperately to think. If she didn't get away from him, she'd explode, but could she just walk out while he lay so still in the bed—and miss her one and only chance to kill him?

Getting control of her consuming rage was the first thing she had to do. Right now she needed time to think. Needed time. Holding her breath, Laurie found a pen and paper and forced herself to scribble the intended message.

At twelve noon I will be at the Herring Inn over windward, just up the coast from the grove of the standing stones. Please join me there for lunch.

Kisses, L.

Their empty sherry glasses were on the bedside table, next to his alarm clock and his watch, the missing aspirin bottle and some loose change. Her shaking hand knocked over a glass when she attempted to prop the note against his clock.

At the loud clink of one glass falling against the other, Eric stirred and opened his eyes. He gazed at her for a moment, then reached toward her. Laurie's only response was a blank stare.

Groggily he asked, "What's the matter? What are you doing?"

"Leaving," she answered. "I was propping a note here on the table. But clumsy me, I knocked over a glass."

"Your voice sounds like that of a stranger, Laurie."

"I . . . I fell asleep. I'm awful when I've just wakened from sleep. I have to get out of here before sunrise."

"Yes, I know." He was barely awake. "What does your note say?"

"It's about lunch. You can read it in the morning."

Laurie quickly slid into her slacks and sweater and started to back out of the room, praying she could stand just a minute or two longer on knees as weak as cotton.

"Aren't you going to kiss me good-night before you disappear?" his groggy voice asked.

She wanted to grab a handful of his thick, dark hair and yank it out of his head. But Laurie's mind had already begun to function again. It would be to her advantage not to let on what she had discovered until she'd had time to absorb it. For her own safety, if nothing else.

Slowly she came forward, leaned over and kissed him lightly on the mouth, expecting the kiss to feel as cold as ice, but his kiss was warm and gentle.

Eric was dozing again when Laurie walked out of his room and into the deathly silent chill of the dimly lighted hallway.

The illusion of love was over.

THE NIGHT WAS exceptionally dark. With only a small lamp burning in her room, Laurie sat propped in her bed, too embroiled in anger and bewilderment to sleep.

How dare he!

Brian was an amateur liar compared to this Englishman. Eric hadn't one sincere bone in his body. He had used her as a guinea pig . . . exposed her to subliminal tapes that he called *their* music, and then systematically recorded her reactions to the subconscious programming. Worst of all, he'd taken complete advantage of his "experiment" by pretending to be in love, so he could seduce her!

How low could a human being sink?

And as for her—how big a fool was it possible to be? Tears streamed down Laurie's cheeks. She'd been naive and stupid about Brian. But this time she'd learned a stark and horrid new meaning of the word "humiliation."

And a new meaning for hurt.

And for loss. Oh, God, she had loved him. Believed him. And believed in her love for him.

"That's it, Laurie V. MacDonald," she whispered viciously through her tears. "*V* for Victim. Damn! I'm going to get you for this you . . . Gypsy . . . or whatever the hell you are! You think you can treat someone who trusts you like this? Someone who cared for you . . . ?"

The silent room filled with her sobs. Tears streaked her cheeks. The trembling only got worse instead of better as the full impact of his deceit enveloped her. "I'll get you for this," she repeated. "I'll make you sorry you ever met me!"

Revenge, she quickly discovered, was the only remedy for heartbreak this deep. Revenge required the energy of the entire body and the cooperation of every cell of the brain. Revenge. She would show him he couldn't get away with using her like this.

But how? She could tamper with his cursed experiment, that's how! Monstrously simple!

It stood to reason that the effectiveness of these subliminal tapes wasn't well determined, for if it had been, Eric wouldn't have been logging every detail of his "subjects'" reactions to hearing them. So no one was sure what the tapes could do. Good! He was about to find out!

"You think life is just a game, do you, Gypsy? Well, you picked the wrong victim this time, because I can play games, too!"

SLEEP was long coming. The ache inside Laurie produced a flow of adrenaline that kept her awake. The only thing that brought her even the slightest cushion of comfort was the realization that within her fertile imagination lurked the ways and means to a workable plan of revenge.

BECAUSE SHE WAS AWAKE nearly all night, Laurie slept through Mrs. Gunn's breakfast hour. She woke, trying to convince herself that last night had been only a nightmare. But the ache in her body was not the residue of a dream. Eric had set her up and used her, and all the wishing in the world couldn't change that.

When she emerged from her room, dressed in slacks and a sweater, Eric's door was closed. He was either asleep or out in the countryside with his recording equipment. No one was in sight downstairs; Mrs. Gunn was doubtless busy in the kitchen or the garden. Marion was probably in her corner of the breakfast room, caught up in a tale of some sordid romantic interlude.

With her notebook and camera beside her, Laurie drove the one-lane cliff road across the northwest corner of the island, trying through a thick layer of pain to think.

The cunning old Druids knew about revenge. And about spells. "Fith-fath," she muttered aloud, her voice rising against the monotonous drone of the car engine. *Fith-fath.* The name of a spell to bring about invisibility, or to change a person into something else. What would she change Eric Sinclair into, if she could? A frog? A slug? An organ grinder's monkey, who broke into a dizzying jig whenever it heard Hungarian Gypsy music?

"Fith-fath." She pulled from her memory a verse so ancient, no one knew from where it came. "A magic cloud I put on thee . . . till I again return." It made a little song for the bumpy road, but only a song. Laurie didn't need the magic of the ancients to wreak well-deserved vengeance on this double-tongued rogue. She had the weapons she needed, and while she was not the professional he was at the art of deceit, she had the best advantage possible. Eric didn't know she knew his secret.

He had set up this despicable game. All she had to do was win!

HERRING INN stood near a grove of trees, at a bend where the road dipped into a shallow glen. Beyond, the moorlands stretched across a terrain inhabited only by sheep. The inn, marked by centuries of harsh weather, was a small, two-story building of whitewashed stone.

When Laurie pulled into the shaded parking lot, Eric's car was already there. She dabbed perfume onto her wrists and quickly ran a brush through her hair.

The dining area was small, with a bar across one end and five tables set about the room, spread with white tablecloths because it was lunchtime. Four of the tables were occupied, one by Eric. He sat sipping a beer, waiting for her.

The sight of him sent a flurry of mixed emotions surging through her. At first she could see only the beauty of him. Dressed in a tan turtleneck sweater, his dark hair curled over his forehead, he was so damned good-looking. His looks made everything too easy for him, and of course he knew it. He took full advantage of his effect upon women. He'd developed the charming personality to match.

In the first mild shock of seeing him, her adoration gave way to sharp stabs of pain and anger as the full impact of his scheme hit her once again. She forced herself to concentrate on the task at hand.

Her trembling was a kind of stage fright. She'd been good at acting in school, and this was going to be no different, she tried to tell herself, except that this time she had the leading role.

And Eric Sinclair for a coach.

He rose when he saw her and came around the table to hold her hand. Knowing that it was inappropriate for this public place, Laurie embraced him and kissed him full on the mouth before she sat down across from him, pretending not to notice that the provocative kiss had attracted the attention of every person in the room.

"I've missed you like crazy," she said.

He smiled. "I've missed you, too. What would you like to drink?"

"Something pink."

"A pink drink? Of what?"

"I don't care, anything. Just so long as it's pink."

"I'll ask." He rose and went to the bar.

Write this down, Eric. The control messages telling your subject she likes pink are taking hold. A few minutes later he returned with something that looked and tasted like a wine cooler.

He watched her closely. "Well? Is it good?"

She nodded. "Lovely color, isn't it? Rather like your shirt—the one you distract people in."

"Do you want to order lunch?"

"There's no hurry, is there?"

"No." Eric sipped his beer. "Discover anything interesting at the standing stones this morning?"

"I can't concentrate on the stones. It's this . . . this *intensity* that overwhelms me. It's you. I can't get you out of mind, Eric, not for a minute. I try to think of other things and it's just no use. Since you made love to me, it's just utterly impossible to function."

"Since we made love to each other," he corrected. "I know. I'm a lost cause myself."

Chin on palms, she gazed up at his eyes, unblinking. "What is this? Is it love?"

"I . . . think it must be," he answered.

"Mmm. Darling, you have the most beautiful eyes. I'll bet people have told you so all your life. I didn't know Gypsies had sky-blue eyes."

"Certainly, some do."

"Those eyes . . . blue pools of magic," she mumbled, staring as if mesmerized until he blinked and glanced sideways.

"Laurie, are you all right?"

"I seem to be in a daze. Oh! Oh, no, don't move! The way the window light touches your face now makes you look like a magnificent painting. Your face is a work of art."

"You're embarrassing me."

"Nonsense. Any man who can hang by his heels in a tavern is not embarrassable."

Eric shifted with obvious discomfort. "What's got into you, love?"

"You. Just big, brawny you." She giggled and sipped pink liquid from her glass.

His gaze met hers. "My question was serious. You're in a damned strange mood."

"Well, I'm . . . smitten. Can I help it if I'm smitten? Isn't it a grand feeling? The way you make love to me proves you're as smitten as I. Aren't we a pair? Laurie and Eric Smitten."

"Good God," he muttered.

She reached across the table to caress his hand, running her forefinger back and forth over his knuckles, transforming each knuckle into a personal keepsake. Under the table her foot played with his ankle.

Small flecks of fire blazed in his eyes. His Adam's apple moved in an involuntary swallow. Laurie noted a slight change in his breathing.

So! Her suggestive touch aroused him! Even when he preferred not to be aroused.

This was valuable information. It moved the contest right onto her turf and gave her a decided advantage, one she hadn't known she could count on. The winds of betrayal were gradually shifting direction.

Laurie advanced without mercy. She wanted to see him writhe. He was uncomfortable already. She was encouraged.

He watched her hand caressing his and didn't move his hand away. Swallowing, he said, "Maybe we should skip lunch."

"And do what?"

"Find our cave."

"Mmm. Yum. I'm starving, though. I've worked up such an appetite this morning."

"Then we'll order. What would you like?"

"Whatever you like."

He frowned. "Fish and chips."

"Fine."

"Black pudding."

"Fine."

"Haggis."

"Fine."

"I hate haggis," he said.

"Me, too. It's made of sheep bladder."

"Laurie. You don't have to eat what I do."

"How else can I demonstrate my adoration of you? Oh, well…" She giggled. "There are ways. I want what you want . . . whatever or wherever. Oh, and I'd love another drink. I don't suppose drinks come in blue. Blue for a boy, pink for a girl. No, I'll stay with pink. I adore pink, don't you? Now, why the heck am I thinking about babies all of a sudden?"

With a strange look on his face, Eric motioned to the waiter and pointed to their glasses. Then he sat rubbing his chin, studying her deeply. "Laurie, have you ever been hypnotized?"

"No. Why would you ask?"

"I think you'd be a hell of a great subject."

Yes, aren't I? she thought. *We've already proven that!* "Me?" she exclaimed. "A subject?" She spat out the word as if it were a worm. "Don't tell me you know how to hypnotize people, darling?"

"I've dabbled in it. It's simpler than most people realize. Want to give it a try sometime?"

She feigned horror. "I'd be scared to death! Why, I'd be completely in your power!"

"People can't be made to do anything they would oppose doing."

"I'd be more interested in hypnotizing *you*."

He laughed. "You do hypnotize me, every time you smile."

"Oh, but I mean really, Eric! If you were completely in my power..." She paused, not trusting herself to look at him. The ice was getting thin here, a little dangerous, but she couldn't resist pushing him out onto it.

"Go on," he insisted. "You'd do what?"

The waiter brought their drinks and took their order for fish and chips. Before he was out of earshot, Laurie answered loudly, "If you were under my power, I'd seduce you right here! No, over there, on the bar."

The waiter stopped, teetered slightly, then walked on without turning back.

Laurie said, "Don't look at me like that, Eric. I wouldn't actually do such a thing—I mean hypnotize you and take unfair advantage. It would be unforgivable! I was only joking. I shouldn't even joke about taking unfair advantage of you. When you're around I can't seem to make myself behave."

His thoughts seemed very far away. A cloud floated across his eyes.

Had her words rooted up some guilt? she wondered. This man? Was he capable of guilt?

She leaned forward. "Is anything wrong, darling? You seem to have suddenly gotten abstracted."

"I'm thinking about you."

"How sweet!" She reached across the narrow table and fondled his ear sensually.

He went a little stiff and said, "We're putting on a show for all the customers. Everybody is looking at us."

"Is it our fault they can't entertain themselves and we can? This little hole in your earlobe is adorable! I can picture a golden earring. . . ."

He grimaced. "Would you mind waiting until after lunch to play with my ear?"

"Tell that to my naughty hands that can't keep away from you. All right, I'll try." She winked at him. "You're being awfully English and disciplined. You showed no such restraint in your bed last night."

His voice dropped several octaves; he was obviously trying to encourage Laurie to lower hers. "I tend to behave differently in restaurants than I do in bed. Call it English reserve, if you like."

"English reserve? I've seen circus clowns more reserved than you. You're probably weak from hunger. Did you have breakfast today?"

"No."

"That explains it. You slept late."

"Not very. I took advantage of the sunshine and drove out to a farm and recorded the roosters crowing."

"Is there a market for rooster crows?"

"A pretty good one. Cows mooing, milk pails clinking—morning sounds on a farm. People enjoy listening to sounds like that, and they can be artistically mixed with music."

Their food was served by the waiter, who gave them curious looks. Laurie ordered another drink.

She was right about his being hungry. They ate in silence for a time, or rather, he ate. Laurie had no appetite for anything but her vengeance. It was hard sitting here, knowing he was amusing himself by thinking what a silly fool she was. This was hard work, but the delicious moments of watching him squirm were worth it. She'd only just begun. He'd programmed her to think she loved him—fine! Love came in many forms.

Suddenly Laurie slammed her fork onto the table. Her eyes blazed. "Eric, how dare you look at that other woman like that! You haven't taken your eyes off of her since we sat down! How can you love me and stare at her? You want her, don't you?"

"What?" He nearly choked on a chip. "What the hell is the matter with you? What other woman?"

"I saw you look at her."

"At who?"

"Who? He dares ask who? The woman at the far table who hasn't taken her eyes off you since we sat down!

You've been staring back at her the whole time. How can you hurt me like that when you know I love you?"

"Your imagination is with the fairies," he answered through gritted teeth. "No man in the world could look at another woman when he's with you."

His words didn't sound like a compliment, but more like a truth he deeply resented. It confused her, but her sense of purpose was undaunted.

"I know what I saw!" Laurie jumped to her feet. "I can't bear to sit here and watch you ogle other women. It hurts too much. Should that be so hard to understand?"

She turned on her heel and walked from the room, through the front door of the inn and into the watery sunshine of early afternoon.

She prayed he wouldn't follow and catch up to her before she got to her car and pulled out onto the road. When she was safely sheltered, she could no longer contain her laughter, but she discovered it was bitter, not sweet.

A glance into the rearview mirror showed her that the way was clear. Eric was probably sitting at the table, finishing his fish and chips under the stares of every pair of eyes in the room. And seething. Knowing he had himself to blame for this, because possessiveness was a part of love's secret persuasion. His best-laid plans were going badly awry.

There were traces of tears in her laughter, and the residue of heartbreak, but it was a release, nevertheless. The therapy of laughter helped to stave off pain. The therapy of fighting helped reduce the sting of humiliation.

Eric had been stunned. Would he stay now? Carry on with his research project? Of course he would. The experiment was going magnificently. Hell, a project this successful deserved national recognition. Subliminal tapes this powerful were worth a fortune for the Aquarius Recording Company. He'd undoubtedly figure a little embarrassment was a small price to pay. The other dividends had been damn good.

Which was another thing. Avoiding sex wasn't going to be easy while she was trying to convince him she was lustfully and shamelessly in love. She needed creativity to work this part out, especially now that she knew how little it took to arouse him. Well, good. Let him pant and sweat while she led him on and then pulled back. Her victory was already beginning to glow in the dying embers of her love.

There was no chance of her coming out of this completely intact, Laurie knew. Subliminally induced or not, she had truly loved him. It wasn't the tapes; they weren't worth a damn. She had realized that at some point during the long, bleak night. She had loved him. She still loved him while she hated him. Love-hate—all one embroiled mixed-up emotion.

Deeply hurt already, Laurie realized she could not come out of this plan of hers without wounds.

But neither would he, Laurie promised herself.

9

ERIC LOST his appetite, but the beer went down fast. He glanced at the woman at the table across the room—the one Laurie had accused him of ogling. She was young and rather pretty; he hadn't noticed her before the tirade. He waved for another beer.

Laurie's behavior was in one sense explicable. In another it wasn't explicable at all. The tapes were programmed to persuade the listener she was in love with whomever she associated that music. Eric believed subliminal programming sometimes brought subtle responses to suggestion.

But this? What the hell had Len put on that tape?

Or was it Laurie? Some people were far more susceptible than others to subconscious suggestion; every researcher knew that. This woman soaked up stimuli like a dry sponge. For all practical purposes she was hypnotized.

Eric concluded that while Laurie was probably a highly suggestive subject, the real cause of her extreme behavior had to be that particular tape.

When Marion had heard it for a relatively short time, she'd begun to act more peculiarly than usual. Seductively, even a little possessively. Laurie had been exposed to hours of that music. Hours. He wondered what Len had done to the original program. Whatever it was, they'd hit a formula that was downright dangerous. They needed to discuss taking these tapes off the market until more data was in, but he knew Len would never listen to him on the matter, unless he had plenty of evidence to back his claims.

Each time he lifted the beer glass, he felt a jab of pain in his wrist, a reminder of his angry attack on the mirror. The pain grated harder on his senses than it did on the injured muscle in his hand. The glass grew lighter as he drank; his mood did not.

There was no point in following Laurie and trying to defend himself against her accusation that he was looking at another woman. She was programmed to want to possess him completely, and nothing else was real to her.

Eric threw pound notes onto the counter and walked outside, though not to his car. He sought solace in the vast emptiness of the moors, but found none. He began to understand it wasn't solace he really wanted— he wanted answers.

He walked the moorlands alone as he had done one summer in his past—the summer he'd run away from the man who claimed to be his father. The summer he'd tried to find his past. The summer he'd spent with the Gypsies, laughed with them, sung with them, and they'd offered him shelter. But he had not belonged to them.

He belonged nowhere.

He took his name from their country, though. That summer with the Scottish tinkers he had randomly chosen the name Sinclair. Before then his father had given him many names to use at various times. His father had at least a dozen surnames. The question of Eric's real name had never been answered.

He was a nobody.

Laurie MacDonald was in love with a nobody.

Her love was as empty and as fleeting as his lies—yet she believed both.

How could truth sprout from the seeds of lies? he asked himself as he walked the rock-hewn hills with the warmth of the sun on his shoulders. He had spoken the truth to her today at least once. *Is it love, Eric?* she had asked. And he had answered, *I think it must be.* God help him, that answer was not a lie when he was speaking for himself.

His love for her was not a lie. Yet a lie was the only reason she loved him. His deceit. A game he'd rushed happily into and now no longer wished to play. But he had no choice. He was in it until the last roll of the dice.

He had to find out how dangerous this game was, how temporary Laurie's state of mind. If things didn't improve, he might have no choice but to try to deprogram her.

And that would mean losing her.

She could never love a man like him for himself, Eric knew. A girl like her could never love a nobody. It was only the tape that had made her love him.

WHEN HE GOT BACK to Dawning Cottage, the three women were having tea in the parlor. It was impossible not to be seen from the front window when he unloaded the recording equipment from his car. He knew they'd be expecting him, even though as often as not he was absent from the four o'clock ritual.

Today, after the disastrous lunch, he wasn't in the mood for socializing. But just inside the hall Laurie was waiting for him.

"Eric," she said. "I forgive you. I've thought it over and I forgive you. I've missed you terribly. I was starting to worry. Where on earth have you been?"

"Counting sheep on the hillsides. Where else would I be? I drove by the standing stones on the way home, thinking you might still be there."

"But that was hours ago."

"Only a couple of hours." He started for the stairs.

She stepped in front of him. "Aren't you having tea?"

"I've got some work to do organizing my—"

"Nonsense," she interrupted, taking his arm possessively. "You can work later. You must have tea because you're an Englishman and it's an English rule."

"The proper Englishman prefers something stronger than tea by four o'clock."

"You're making that up, Eric." As she proceeded to urge him toward the parlor, Marion was suddenly on his opposite arm. One woman was pulling, the other hanging.

"Eric for tea!" Marion announced to Jeanne Gunn, who proceeded to pour.

"All right! Fine," he conceded. "Just give me a chance to unload." He set his recorder and microphones and a box of tapes on the hall table.

The sitting room was comfortable without a fire because the day had been sunny. The usual assortment of pastries were set out with care. Laurie appeared relaxed, but Marion was swooping around like a hawk searching for movement in the long grass. How was he

going to deal with both of them—one whom he loved
and the other whom he could barely tolerate? That
Jeanne Gunn hadn't been in the room yesterday afternoon when Laurie played his tape must have been a
merciful act from heaven, although he wasn't sure if he
deserved it.

Bracing himself, Eric accepted the tea, and sat down
in front of the tray of sweets. "Mrs. Gunn, the man is
yet to be born who could resist your fresh raspberry
tarts."

"Have your fill, lad," his hostess said with a smile.
"And how's the work progressin'?"

"Well enough to take me away from Lees before too
much longer."

Marion's hand moved to her breast. "Don't say that!
Without your voice, these echoing halls will be empty
as the wind across the braes!"

Laurie looked at her incredulously, blinked twice and
then amended, "Yes, empty as that still, hollow hour
just before the dawn."

Jeanne Gunn stared at the two women.

"What's been going on here?" Eric asked.

Marion clinked her cup upon the saucer. "Why, to
confess, we have been discussing you. Miss Mac-
Donald insists the flecks in your eyes are silver and I insist they are gold. Who is right?"

He took a huge bite of the sweet tart, trying to convince himself it was too soon for full-throttle panic.
Panic was a fault he reserved for weaker men. Eric was
accustomed to being in control, but his confidence was
crumbling minute by minute.

Something told him that Laurie and Marion were glaring at each other behind his back. *I've been in worse predicaments than this*, he reminded himself fiercely. But at that moment he couldn't name a single one of them. The scent of perfume permeated the small room—two distinct fragrances at war with each other. One was heavy musk, the other an overpowering flower scent. He'd never been aware of either woman using too much perfume before today, but the poorly blending scents were getting to him. The room smelled like a cheap brothel.

Humming a melody from the infamous tape, Laurie took a bite of chocolate cream, then reached out and thrust the rest of the biscuit toward him. "Try this yummy thing."

But instead of the little cookie Eric felt her finger in his mouth.

"Don't bite me, Eric!"

"How could he help it?" Marion asked. She sat like a statue in her favorite chair, smoothing a linen serviette over her knees. Her eyes were glowing like hot coals.

Laurie was moving her fingers along his teeth. Gently he extracted her hand from his mouth, weak with embarrassment, more for her than for himself. "You're in a mood," he muttered.

"Do you know what I wish?" she asked, moving her forefinger teasingly along his shoulder. "I wish you'd worn your pink shirt. It suits you."

"Pink doesn't suit me."

"Ah, but pink does. Sunrises are pink and the sun sets pink. I'll always think of you every time I see a pink sunset. No, I'll think of you in pink candlelight. Or sometimes I'll see you in a pink shirt playing a game and winning, because you always win."

Jeanne Gunn interrupted. "Laurie, is something the matter?"

Laurie frowned, then smiled. "I didn't sleep well last night and woke feeling giddy, and the giddiness just won't go away. I don't know what's causing it." She shot Eric a glance full of meaning. "Do you?" she whispered coyly.

Eric muttered the first senseless words that formed in his brain. "The elevated latitude might explain it."

Jeanne's eyebrows rose. "Latitude?"

"Altitude," Marion corrected. "Elevated altitude is what he said."

"I didn't say altitude. Latitude sickness is hard to diagnose because it's slow to make itself felt."

Jeanne, who had a strong aversion both to madness and the level of tension in this room, set down her cup and rose. "I must check my tomato plants." She exited abruptly.

Laurie spoke up. "Eric, latitudes are the horizontal lines, aren't they? I always have to stop and think. Yes, horizontal. But of course you'd be thinking horizontally. What do you mean latitude sickness? Who has ever heard of such a thing?"

He tried to decide whether or not to answer. Laurie was acting so flightily that he couldn't tell how much was her sarcastic humor and how much illusion. He'd begun the nonsense to divert attention from himself, but now he didn't know where to go with it. He had to get Laurie alone to talk—if he dared be alone with her, and if talking would do any good at this stage of her emotional deterioration.

"We're at high latitudes here," he said finally. "Tends to make one light-headed."

Laurie raised her hand to her brow, palm out. "Oh Eric, Eric, Eric. How I love your sense of the ridiculous!"

"He's having us on," Marion said. "Beastly, that!"

"You're having us on," Laurie repeated. "Which might offend Maid Marion, but you can have *me* on *anytime*."

"I can't stand this," Eric said. His face was grim.

Marion's voice rose. "I say, Laurie, you're starting to make a fool of yourself."

"Am I? Well, good heavens, I never start something I can't finish."

She moved around to the back of Eric's chair and began to rub his shoulder. "Our lad seems horribly tense. I noticed it at lunch. But we won't get into that ugly matter."

Her fingers moved along his shoulders and neck and came finally to his ear, which she caressed with little circles of love. *Not the ear again*, he thought desperately. It didn't seem to bother Laurie in the least that Marion was sitting there with the face of someone being forced to watch a postmortem, while drumming her fingers on the arms of her chair.

He thought of a blue film he'd seen once, in which a man was handcuffed naked to a bed and tickled mercilessly with peacock feathers while he writhed helplessly. In his mind he was that victim—helpless because he cared too much for Laurie to say anything to further humiliate her. Especially while the overreactive, half-programmed Miss Huckles DuBois was taking in every one of his breaths as if they were her own.

He wasn't, after all, Laurie's victim. He was a victim of his own ill-fated game. So was she. So was poor confused Marion. Eric fought his anger, fought for self-control and groped for answers.

She had gone from the ear back to her fascination with his knuckles. Surely Len hadn't put this stuff onto the tape!

With closed eyes, studying his hand as if she were blind and her fingers were her eyes, Laurie said, "There are no two knuckles alike. I would recognize yours anywhere, even in the dark."

"Good God, Laurie!"

"What?" Her eyes opened. She looked around, dazedly. Then, "Marion, what are you doing? Are you taking notes?"

"I'm trying to work on my book in this shockingly bawdy atmosphere."

"Get off it, Marion! You're taking notes!"

"Well, what could you expect, since you insist on provoking a professional writer of romance to the absolute limits. It's like wriggling a mouse in front of a spirited cat. Speaking metaphorically, as a writer must."

"You're writing a description of Eric's knuckles. Don't deny it."

"That does it!" Eric leaped up like a man who had been sitting on a hot coal that had just smoldered through and ignited his pants. "Laurie, what the hell is going on?"

She drew back. "What do you mean? Oh, my, I didn't mean to embarrass you. I don't know what's happening to me, Eric. I'm acting like an absolute idiot, aren't I? I can't seem to get control of my impulses, and all my impulses seem to be directed to . . . to you."

"Anyone can plainly see that," Marion put in, making another quick notation on her page.

Marion's writing bothered Laurie. Even though she herself was playacting, the note taking was an invasion of privacy. Leaning on the mantel, she held both hands to her forehead. "I don't feel well. I'm sure I have that latitude condition."

Eric took a step forward. He had to separate Laurie and Marion.

"Eric, watch out!" Marion shrieked as his leg caught the corner of the tea tray that extended out over the edge of the low table. The tray slid forward. Little round cookies and the two remaining raspberry tarts began to dance as the tray teetered.

The shudder and shifting of the platter knocked over a teacup. It came crashing down onto the falling tray. With quick reflexes, Eric reached to catch the treasured, hand-painted china plate that served as Mrs. Gunn's tea tray. One of his thumbs sank deeply into a berry tart, the other slid across the sharp edge of the broken cup.

Uttering an oath, he replaced the platter safely on the table. The tray's contents were askew, floating in spilled tea that was streaked with the red of his blood.

He stood stunned, both red thumbs in the air.

"Horror, you're hurt!" Marion scurried about with urgency as if his life were ebbing away. She produced a perfumed handkerchief with which she attempted to blot at first one thumb, then the other.

"It's no more than a small cut," he said impatiently, taking the handkerchief from her. "It's nothing."

"Nothing? Both of your thumbs are bleeding and you say it's nothing?"

"This one is raspberry juice, Marion."

Laurie had watched the accident without moving a muscle. Now she cocked her head sideways as he dabbed at the little wound. "Fee fi fo fum! I smell the blood of an Englishman!"

Eric looked up, simply looked at her blankly until he blinked. "Laurie, perhaps you should lie down."

"Too dangerous. Every time I lie down I get into trouble."

His pride couldn't take any more. "You won't get into trouble," he said slowly, as if he were talking to someone who could barely comprehend the English language. He meant every word. He could not make love to her again; it wouldn't happen. His honor—what little honor he could salvage now—would not allow it.

How he was going to avoid their lovemaking, though, was going to be a difficult challenge—especially since he wanted to make love to Laurie until she loved him and not the stupid tape. "I want to talk to you," he said. "I'm going out to the garden. I want to talk to you in the garden."

He felt the glare of Marion's eyes, but it couldn't be helped. Without a word he handed her back her stained handkerchief.

Outside in the front garden, Laurie grabbed his hand and licked the raspberry away, nibbling like a hungry mouse. He resisted yelling at her, but it wasn't easy. She deserved pity, not impatience.

Eric turned on the garden hose and held it over his hands. The cold water stopped the bleeding. He shook his head. "Fee fi fo fum?"

She giggled. "I'll bet that comes from 'fith-fath.' I thought about it earlier. Do you know about 'fith-fath'?"

"I know about curses," he answered. "It's the name of a curse."

"I had no idea until I came here that it's pronounced 'fee-fa.' What do you know about these ancient things?"

"I've already told you I believe in most of them."

"Oh, yes. Well, I never know if you're serious. Except about loving me. I was kidding about feeling ill. I knew I was behaving rather oddly, because of feeling so happy inside, because of you loving me. I didn't want to lord our happiness over poor little you-know-who. Only..."

He drank from the garden hose, then laid it down in a flower bed and wiped his chin. "Only what?"

"Only I wish you wouldn't look at her."

"Look at Marion?"

"I can't bear it if you look at another woman. Promise you'll never look at another woman as long as we both live."

"That's a long time to keep my eyes focused straight ahead at the wall."

"If you love me, you'll promise."

He stepped into the mud of the flower bed, shook his foot, and began scraping his shoe on the grass. He had sunk in all the way to his sock.

"You're awfully clumsy today, Eric. Is it my fault?"

"I'd be lying if I said it wasn't."

"I know exactly how you feel. Isn't it wonderful?"

"Laurie, we have to talk."

"Of course. There's so much to talk about. What shall we talk about first?"

He paused, stopped dead by an impenetrable wall of deceit. What the hell was he supposed to say to her?

The truth?

He didn't dare. Not until he somehow determined how much trouble she was really in. He had to try to deprogram her, and that wouldn't be possible if she knew what he was doing. The truth in this case would not set her free; the truth would only tighten the wires of the trap he'd set for her.

She was humming one of the melodies from the tape again while she watched him scrape mud off his shoe. "Well?" she asked. "Are we talking yet?"

"I just wanted to ask you to explain to me why you're so obsessed with my knuckles."

Disappointment clouded her face. "Oh, that. I can't explain it. I just appreciate every wonderful inch of you. Your knuckles each have little individual faces and wrinkly bumps that are you and you alone."

He could not hide the grimace. "Laurie. I can't stand any more of that. I'm serious—I can't take it. Damn it, try to think of something else. Think about what we're having for dinner or something."

"I'm having that last thumb-flavored tart."

"Stop it!" He paused, looking stricken. "Please."

She touched his arm. "Oh, Eric! What's wrong?"

"I don't feel well."

"You don't look well, but you actually lost very little blood."

If he didn't get away from this woman, at least for a few minutes, he was going to lose it. What in the name of heaven had he done to her?

"Laurie, you'll have to excuse me. I'm going to make a phone call. Business. Some matters I have to talk over with my business partner."

"But we were going to talk. You were about to ask me to marry you."

His eyes closed in private pain, then opened again. "We'll talk soon."

"Oh, well, all right, if you can stand to be in suspense over what my answer will be."

Eric made his way into the house, thankful that Laurie had chosen to stay in the garden, in the fresh air she needed so badly.

He dialed London.

"Len," he said. "The situation here is highly disturbing. The experiment with the subliminal love tape has gone berserk."

"What'd you do, forget to log?"

"I logged until yesterday. Now everything is . . . it's insane. Listen, Len, these tapes are dangerous."

His partner's voice cracked. "What are you talking about?"

"You'll just have to take my word for it until I have a chance to explain. We've got to take those tapes off the market."

"Have you gone mad? After what we've invested in this equipment? Sales on them are just beginning to show a profit, and their future looks more promising than anything else we've got."

"I know all that. But the stimuli are too damned strong. What did you do to that program, for God's sake?"

"Come on! No data has ever suggested anything dangerous. We're talking about love here! Most testers say the tapes have little effect at all."

"They weren't testing our tape. Len, I don't think we'd better sell these until we have more data on what we've really got here."

The other man's voice sounded as though he had lost patience. "I've never known you to get hysterical before, mate. Come on home. We'll talk about it."

"Can't. I can't just leave this thing hanging."

"Right, then. You get it together out there, then come in and we'll go over this—nice and calmlike. There's a tad of panic in your voice."

"Did you ever know me to panic without a reason?"

"Hell, I never knew you to panic with a reason. Tell me what happened."

"All I can tell you is, the stimuli are too strong. This woman is in a posthypnotic state, and I don't know how to get her out of it."

"Bloody hell! You mean she's—"

"I can't talk about it now. Just consider this a red alert. We're handling a dangerous weapon, Len. I'll get back when I can. Don't play around in the studio anymore. I don't know what you did, but don't do it anymore."

Laurie came into the house as Eric hung up the phone, but she didn't see him in the shadowy hallway.

She seemed in a great hurry, bounding up the stairs as if there were something on her mind that couldn't wait.

She's heading for my room, Eric thought. With sweat trickling down his back, he shot out of the front door and into his car.

Running from a beautiful woman desperate for his body. How could his life have ever come to this?

No, he realized, he was running from himself. If he were alone with her, he wouldn't be able to resist her. He couldn't before; he couldn't now. All she had to do was look at him, and he was lost.

10

SHE WASN'T through with him yet. The score was far from even. A bizarre idea had wakened Laurie in the night. One grand play, she decided. One last "gift" to leave him. Then she would depart forever from this island with its thousand hurtful memories.

It wouldn't take long to finish gathering her data at the Druid sacrificial site. The ways of the Druids were magical, full of horror and of beauty, and the legacy of the strange Gypsy who understood those ways better than an ordinary man should. He was not a man to betray. Eric Sinclair could be dangerous to a person who turned on him; of this she was certain. But her anger overpowered the fear.

Revenge generated its own energy as no other emotion could, and her pride needed it. But revenge was not as sweet as it ought to be. Watching Eric squirm with discomfort was good for a bruised heart, but the same bruised heart that had loved him was unable to cast off her love as if it had never existed.

She felt the pain of that love during the drive into Fyfe's Landing the next day in late morning. The strain of deceit was taking its toll on her nerves. Deceit was no threat to Eric's health; he clearly throve on it, but for her each small victory had a sharp, double edge. Each lie cut her while it was cutting him. His lies were a way of life; hers were a way of survival.

And a part of her still loved a part of him—the unreachable part that she would never have a chance to know.

This cloudy Saturday morning the villagers were wearing heavy woolen sweaters on the streets of Fyfe's Landing. Wind blew cold off the waters of the harbor. Laurie parked her car in front of a small dry goods shop on the town's single commercial street, and buttoned her jacket against the wind.

Behind her at the water's edge, a few fishing boats pulled restlessly at their moorings. Children were darting back and forth along the docks in a game of tag, their shouts mingling with the mellow squawks of sea gulls flying overhead.

Sea gulls. The ancients believed they were the souls of the dead. Appropriate somehow, Laurie thought. She was partly dead herself, now that what little she had left of trust had been stolen from her. The gulls cried like the emptiness inside her cried—a soul in search of itself....

The sign was here someplace, in the corner of a salt-stained window of one of these little shops. She'd happened to see it after the ferry ride over to Lees, those few days and forever ago, before she had ever heard of Eric Sinclair.

Many voices, Scottish voices, sounded from the town's one tavern, midway down the street. Laurie followed the voices on instinct, and sure enough, the tavern was the establishment she was looking for. Mist that was almost rain felt cold on her face as she stood at the window of the tavern, gazing at a faded sign with only one word in weak, black letters: Tattoos. The sign appeared to have been in that window for half a century, but since no one had removed it, there must be a tattoo artist on the premises.

Heads turned toward her as she walked into the smallest tavern she had ever seen. More than half a dozen customers stood at the bar at high noon. Not one of them was a woman.

She stepped to the corner of the bar. "I noticed the sign in your window," she said to the bartender. "Is there a tattoo artist here?"

The man's face registered surprise. "Aye, we've a man in Fyfe's who once worked that trade in Glasgow."

She set her handbag upon the bar. "Does he still do tattoos?"

"I'm told he's still in business, though the old boy likely hasna taken his needles out for a dozen years. Not much demand for tattoos here on Lees. His name's MacNeil. Just turn to your right at the end of this street, this side of the greengrocer's, go on up Hillbrow Street until ye reach number nine, and that'll be his house. Wee, gray house." He gazed at her with restrained curiosity. "Surely it wouldna be for ye, lass?"

"I just want to talk to him."

"Todd MacNeil will make ye welcome."

"Thanks. Thank you very much."

Whispers would fill the silence left by her exit, she knew. Hers was a puzzling request from an American tourist, a woman alone. None of that was important. Only her mission mattered . . . her creatively devastating way to convince Eric Sinclair that she was hopelessly in love with him.

LAURIE STOOD in her underwear in front of the mirror in her bedroom, admiring Todd MacNeil's work. Her outfit for tonight was carefully planned. It was cold to wear a short-sleeved blouse, but she would wear one, anyway. Things would heat up fast enough when she entered the dining room.

She had made two more stops in the village before coming back. A cup of tea in the tearoom to calm down after leaving MacNeil, and a visit to the little dry goods shop, where she'd found a pink-dotted scarf. Jeanne and Marion and Eric would have assumed she'd been at the standing stones all day.

She decided on a white blouse, and rolled up the sleeves so her arms would be bare. The entire tattoo had to be in plain view. Turning in the light, she admired the outline of a pink heart bordered by roses with four bold letters in the center: Eric. MacNeil had proved to be a talented artist.

Explaining what she wanted hadn't been as difficult as she'd feared it might be. The old man, rugged and weathered, who had lived much of his life on the seafront, asked no questions. Aye, he had answered her, the ink was almost indelible, and aye, he could make it look just as genuine using ink without the needles. And aye, this ink would take upwards of two weeks to wash off, even with scrubbing. No one could distinguish his drawing from an actual tattoo; this he guaranteed.

MacNeil had made the stem of the rose resemble a snake, so that when scrutinized, the design of rose and heart took on a sinister, if not evil, appearance. It was perfect.

Now to do something with her hair.

Five minutes before time to go down to the dining room, she heard a knock. Laurie grabbed her jacket just before the door opened.

"Laurie? Are you ready for dinner?"

"Oh, darling, I'm not late, am I?"

He stepped into the room, only to stop short as soon as he saw her. "You look different. Your hair."

"Like it?"

"Uh . . . it's sort of . . . in your face. Can you see all right?"

"This is my new look . . . for you. Does it give the impression I'm just off a warm bed? It took me an hour to do it so it looks like it hasn't been combed. I knew you'd like the sensual look."

"You were gone all day," he said quickly. "I missed you."

"Oh, I missed you, too. I drove into the village. I found this pretty pink scarf. . . ." She was watching his eyes, using powers of her own to put him off balance. Gazing up at him, she drew the scarf slowly across her face and licked her lips provocatively.

His reaction was instant. He swept her into his arms and kissed her.

She was left weak and fluttery. Even when she fought it, his kisses could arouse her. It was dangerous to be alone with him. Thank God, Jeanne Gunn was waiting for them this very minute. But the way he had kissed her, Eric wasn't going to be the least concerned whether they got down to dinner or not. His lips were moving over her neck, while he pushed the loose strands of hair away from her face.

There was one fast way to stop him.

"Oh, Eric, I want to show you the proof of my love."

"Yes, my sweet . . ." he mumbled through the kisses.

"Under my jacket."

He slid the heavy blue cardigan from her shoulders and tossed it onto the bed. Laurie pulled out of his embrace and turned so the light would shine upon her arm.

"Look, Eric!"

He caught his breath in disbelief so complete that he started to choke. His lips opened, but only gasps came out. While Laurie watched, his face paled to white.

He was unable to speak.

She smiled mischievously. "There is a tattoo artist in Fyfe's Landing. I thought, what better remembrance of our nights of love than this? At first I thought of putting your name on my chest, next to my heart, but then I decided, no, I want it on my arm, where the whole world can see it!" She paused. "Eric? Are you all right?"

He had stumbled back. Now he was sitting on the edge of the bed, looking sicker than the night he'd been unconscious.

"A tattoo? How could you do this?"

"You're pleased, aren't you, darling? This way everyone will always know that I belong to you."

"Why would you . . . ?" His voice was becoming weaker by the moment. "Why would you think of a tattoo, for God's sake?"

"Why? Because I'm so in love with you I felt compelled to wear your name. Such a deep compulsion . . . like a voice from somewhere, telling me over and over how much I love you. You look sick, darling. What is it?"

His head was buried in his hands. "You're right. I don't feel well."

"Oh, dear! I should be more sensitive to your feelings! Here I am, going on and on about my tattoo, when you are feeling ill! How selfish of me. I'm not good enough for you, Eric, I'm really not. Here, let me help you. Don't you want to lie down? What can I get for you?" She moved toward him, her voice crooning. "I'll take care of you. I'll always be right there to take care of you."

When she reached down to assist him onto the pillow, Eric grasped her arm and held it in front of him, studying the tattoo like a condemned man reading his own death sentence.

She whispered, "Don't you love the way the stem of the rose becomes a winding little snake?"

"I can't believe you did this."

"I'm terribly proud of it."

He released her hand, doubled over as if he were suffering stomach cramps and dropped his head into his palms.

"You're in crash position!" she said.

"I think I'm going to be sick."

"It's all right, I'm here."

"No, it isn't all right. I'm not going to be sick in front of you. I'm going to my room. You go down to dinner and give my regrets to Jeanne. Please. With your cardigan on."

"I couldn't leave you!"

"Please," he repeated. He rose stiffly and started for the door. "Don't fuss over me. I'm not a man who likes being fussed over. Just . . . I have to be alone for a little while, Laurie. I've got to decide what to do."

He opened the door, then turned back. "Roll down your sleeves. If Jeanne and Marion see your arm, we'll probably be asked to leave."

"I never thought of that!"

He nodded weakly. "Meet me after supper."

"Shall I come to your room?"

"No. I'll wait for you outside, on the cliff over the waterfall."

"Okay. Don't get too close to the edge."

But they were both too close to the edge, she knew. The tattoo had worked. Boy, had it worked! She could hold her own in this vicious game.

But she didn't have to like it. Softness had gone from her life when the joy left. A woman's heart that has truly loved never forgets the softness and the joy—the tender moments no one else would ever know about.

Laurie couldn't forget, even now.

TWILIGHT HUNG in the sky until midnight. The air was cool on the moors in the long, eerie evenings. Night sounds with no night. An impotent moon trying to rule a night without darkness. The sea, contentedly breathing against the cliffs through the daylight hours, sounded angry behind the ghostly shades of twilight.

The moors at twilight frightened Laurie. Loneliness resided here. The creeping mist, cries of gulls, the distant growl of the ill-natured sea. Unexplained shadows.

Walking in wet grass down the slope of the garden and up the rising terrain toward the ridge of the hill, she felt part of the loneliness that extended across these grim and untamed hills. Only the wild daisies were friendly. They popped out of the grass like little smiles, undaunted by the forbidding press of twilight.

Eric's form was silhouetted against the sky as he stood on the brow of the hill among the outlines of grizzled trees. So tall and husky—perfect male beauty.

Life isn't fair, Laurie whispered to the indifferent wind. Because the wiles of men dominated it, life would never be fair.

He turned and walked down from the crest to meet her, his hair blowing over his forehead, his sweater sleeves pushed up on bare forearms as if he could not feel the cold.

Without a word he took her hand and led her to where the stone wall curved, so they could sit and look out at the ocean.

Still without a word, he leaned over and kissed her, first her cheek and then her lips.

"You deserve better than me."

"Why would you say that?" she asked.

"I say it because it's the truth. Sometimes I tell the truth." He looked down at the stone he was digging up with his heel. "Look, Laurie, infatuation is . . . can be a powerful thing. But it's not the same as love. You're infatuated with me. . . ."

"You can say that again." She smiled.

"It isn't real love, though," he answered weakly.

"Oh, come on! If this isn't love, then there is no such thing as love. You're infatuated with me, aren't you?"

"Yes."

"You're saying you don't love me!"

"No, that isn't what I meant."

"What do you mean then?"

He dug at another rock and didn't answer.

Laurie touched his knee. "Did you want to meet me just to tell me I don't love you after I've just proved it?"

His eyes remained on the ground; his voice was barely audible. "I don't know what to say, damn it."

"You might be sweet and tell me how much you love our tattoo. My special tribute to you."

"I can't believe you did that."

"What? I can barely hear you. Why are you whispering?"

He finally looked at her. "Laurie, I have to ask you something. How much did you listen to my tape? Did you play it at night when you were sleeping?"

"I went to sleep to it. Why?"

"There's another tape I'd like to get for you."

What's this one? she wondered. *Erotic stuff, probably, since he thought the damn thing worked so well. Did he have no conscience at all?* "No," she replied, pouting. "I want the old one. I want it back. Why can't you make me a copy?"

"I lost it," he said.

"Lost? How could you possibly? It has to be in your room somewhere."

"I brought it out here, and the wind blew it out of my hand and took it over the cliff."

She stared at him. "That's utterly preposterous!"

"I know. Freak accident. It's been washed out to sea."

"What kind of complete idiot do you take me for?"

"Hell, it's only a tape. Let's just forget it."

When she reached over to caress his knuckles, she felt his hand trembling. Eric was a nervous wreck tonight. Good. She patted his arm affectionately. "Why don't we go over to the Red Wolf? Just to socialize and have a drink. Show off my tattoo."

"Oh, God."

"You don't want to go?"

"I'd rather not."

"If I promised to leave your ears alone, would you go?"

"Would you promise to be good?"

She nodded with a sigh. "Is it my fault I can't keep my hands off you? No, it's your fault for being irresistible. Let's go have lots of drinks. I want to lose my inhibitions."

"My sweet, if you lose any more inhibitions, Marion will have enough material for three sequels."

She giggled. "DuBois writes only personal experiences. She told me so."

"Sure."

"You don't believe her. Why not?"

"Because I'm a man."

She grasped his arm. "Oh, heavens, that publisher is also a man! Suppose he doesn't believe her, either? He'll be here tomorrow! Marion was ecstatic at dinner, saying her book is going to tilt the earth on its axis. The publisher wants to promote *her* along with her scandalous memoirs in a great publicity campaign."

"She's a fraud," he said. "And not even a clever one."

"You don't like her."

"It's quite mutual."

"She seems enchanted with you at times. And I think she expected you to be under her spell."

Eric smiled.

"She *did*, didn't she?"

"Yes, ridiculous as that sounds. She's a good twenty years older than I'll ever be."

"Poor Marion."

"Bosh. The woman is her own problem. She's not going to fool that publisher for a second."

Misty silence settled over them once again. Laurie caressed his arm and he caressed hers back, lovingly. Now and then his hand would move over the tattoo and under her sweater; his hand would pause there and he would lapse into strained silence. The Red Wolf was forgotten.

At length she said, "It's getting a bit cold out here."

His arm came around her and he kissed her.

He whispered, "I'm sorry, Laurie."

"For the weather?"

His only answer was a bearlike embrace, in which he held her solidly against him, shielding her from the night. The embrace robbed her of her breath, not because it was too tight, but because, swallowed by the warmth of him, she felt protected. It was almost as if the man were protecting her from himself!

"You're cold. We'd better go in."

When she didn't respond or move, he said, "You're frightened of something. What is it?"

"The twilight shadows," she lied, because she could not admit to Eric that it was the nearness of him that scared her. "Your little nature spirits are all around us tonight. I can feel them."

"They come out at twilight. But don't worry, they won't harm you. I won't let them."

"Can they harm me if I don't believe in them?"

"Oh, yes. But they won't."

She nestled against him. "Do you really believe in the fairies and brownies? I mean truly?"

"Yes."

"Because you're a Gypsy?"

"I don't know."

"It's a . . . an obsolete . . . religion."

He smiled. "You've been on this island long enough to know it isn't dead and never will be."

For a reason she couldn't comprehend, Laurie felt close to tears. "I don't understand you," she said. "Eric, I just don't understand you. You say you believe in fairies . . . and yet you're . . ."

Reading her mind again, he answered, "They're not all good fairies. You keep forgetting that. Some of them are downright dangerous."

"Like you."

"Yes, unfortunately."

She caught her breath. "Should I be afraid of you?"

"Yes."

She fell into a deadly silence.

A sea gull circled over their heads, crying mournfully. The wind blew her hair around her face. Her silence asked why, but it was a long time before he answered the question she was afraid to voice.

"Because of who I am," he said.

She looked at his silver-blue eyes. "Who are you, Eric?"

The blue eyes looked out toward the solitary, haunted hills. "I don't know," was all he said.

Who this man is, Laurie thought with an agonizing ache in her heart, *who this man is, I'll never know. If life were kinder I'd forget him someday, but I won't forget him, ever.*

Real tattoos scarred badly when they were surgically removed. The scars of this one would go far deeper. The horrible game they were playing hurt too much. The sooner she got away from Eric, the better.

THEY RETURNED to find a bustle of activity in the parlor. Jeanne Gunn and Marion were making preparations for tomorrow's important guest, Mr. Pennington of Pennington and Harkborne, Publishers.

Laurie eagerly offered to help. It was her excuse for not going upstairs, where, no doubt, Eric planned to lure her into his lair again. To her surprise, he did nothing to try to get her up there. The last thing he seemed to want was scandalous gossip in the house. That was understandable, considering the fact that he was an Englishman.

THE FOLLOWING MORNING was no ordinary one at Dawning Cottage. Tension ran high. Breakfast was a test of nerves. Marion as a prima donna was not easy to take. Her entrance fifteen minutes late was drama at its worst. Wearing a long-sleeved, red crepe dress that hung shapelessly from her thin shoulders, she paused in the doorway with the forced tolerance of a queen surveying her subjects.

Marion in red was not an improvement. It paled her skin and sharpened her birdlike features. As always, her gray-streaked hair was pulled back severely from her face. Today she wore a pair of small, green jade earrings. Laurie marveled at the total picture, for even in the way she dressed, Marion never stopped contradicting herself.

"My last days with my dear friends of Lees," she sang, sweeping to a place at the table. "This morning I shall not sit at my usual sunny window. I shall sit with all of you."

"Where are you going after today?" Jeanne Gunn asked.

"Why, to London, of course. To the hub of the world of publishing. But I shall take memories with me of this lovely cottage from where my talent was first discovered."

"Maybe Jeanne ought to put a plaque up over the door," Eric said sourly, popping a bite of kipper into his mouth.

Marion watched her hostess pour tea. "In actual fact, a plaque will be there someday. People will ask to see the rooms where I wrote. It will be fine for you, Jeanne. Dawning will be on the map. No more obscurity for the little island of Lees. I feel quite good about that."

"Isn't this all a little premature?" Eric asked. "Considering you've never sold one bloody word?"

She glared at him. "You, Mr. Sinclair, are unpresentable. Not only at breakfast in the presence of women, but shockingly inappropriate to meet my publisher. That scruffy pullover. And unshaven. This is not acceptable. I can't have my publisher thinking I associate with ruffians."

"The laddie has been on the moors this fine morning," Jeanne Gunn said, squinting at the author as if she were trying to bring her into sharper focus.

Eric smiled. "I thank you, Mrs. Gunn, but I've no need for alibis. No disrespect intended to you, Miss Huckles, but I'll dress as I bloody choose."

Marion sucked in her breath.

Laurie tried to suppress a smile. Marion's adoration of Eric had obviously worn off. "When does your publisher arrive?"

"The ferry from the mainland docks at nine o'clock," Jeanne answered. "Add the drive to here from Fyfe's Landing, and that should get him to Dawning well before ten."

"Ten," Marion repeated. "You won't be ready, Jeanne! What are you serving besides scones and tea cakes? Shouldn't there be cucumber sandwiches? And I've been thinking about the lunch menu. Lamb chops seem so mundanely rural. Can't you do something more Continental?"

"We're not on the Continent." Jeanne scowled. "The man will eat my lamb chops or he'll have nothing."

"There must be fresh flowers on the table. You will have time to cut the flowers, won't you?"

"Try to calm yourself, Marion," Laurie said. "We'll be ready. We'll all help."

"All but the ruffian," Eric said, pushing away from the table. "I've got more frivolous things to do with my time."

"Someday," Marion hissed, "you will be bragging to people that you knew me once, and when they ask I'll say I can't remember you."

He leaned on the back of his chair. "My dear Miss Huckles, rarely have I met a human being with conceit as overbearing as yours. The swank in this room is making the air too thick to breathe." He turned and left.

The silence was deafening. At last Marion said, "He is cruel. Jealous and cruel. I shan't let the likes of that tinker person spoil the most important day of my life."

Eric was good at spoiling days, Laurie thought. But in this instance his impatience was justified.

AT NINE FORTY-FIVE the car arrived. Not one, but two men appeared at the door of Dawning, the older in a stiff gray suit, the other immaculate in a medium brown coat over dark brown slacks, a silk paisley scarf at his neck.

The sitting room was freshly dusted and fragrant with the perfume of flowers in glass vases. Because the day was warm, the windows were open and a light sea breeze moved the lace curtains. Mrs. Gunn, in her Sunday dress, led the guests into the room where Marion sat at center stage. Laurie was on the sofa to lend her support.

Marion rose with rehearsed flourish and extended her hand, palm down and limp, expecting it to be retrieved in the course of a gentleman's bow.

Laurie's heart leaped into her throat. She was insane to allow herself to suffer this kind of tension. The faces of the men froze at the first sight of Marion. Both gaped.

Then in unison their eyes moved over the room toward Laurie.

In unison their faces relaxed and smiled.

"Miss DuBois!" the younger publisher said, extending his hand to Laurie. "This is indeed a pleasure!"

11

LAURIE FELT the color drain from her face. "Oh, no! No, I'm not Margo DuBois." She gestured toward the woman in red crepe who stood posed before the mantel.

Together they turned again. The silence was horrible.

Finally the older spoke. "Miss DuBois, I am Harold Pennington. This is Jonathan Bottoms, one of our publicity people."

"An honor, gentlemen. Please sit down. Are you tired from your journey? I trust the sea was not rough this morning." Marion spoke as if she didn't sense their confusion.

They sat. Neither was smiling.

"We found your manuscript quite interesting, as you know," Pennington began without prolonging the niceties any further. "We felt it has certain commercial possibilities because of its, shall we say, insight into the mind of a woman who lives her romantic fantasies in her real life...." The man's voice cracked. His expression became squeamish as he looked at her, the way one does after witnessing a grim accident, expecting to see casualties.

Marion smiled demurely and sat down across from him, hands in her lap.

"I say, Miss DuBois. You did claim this book is fact."

"Of course."

Bottoms cleared his throat. "We've discussed publicity for this project based on personal appearances, presenting the author as a sexy, outrageously outspoken woman whom no man can resist," he said in a hard, businesslike voice. "Which is the way you presented yourself, Miss DuBois."

"Quite so."

Laurie squirmed with discomfort. *Marion is finished,* she thought. Their first look had said it all.

Pennington twisted his ring annoyingly. "You understand that we feel the book can't stand on its own without an identity for the author. We need a personality who can tantalize, making this book believable, and quite frankly, Miss DuBois, you're not the kind of person we anticipated meeting."

Laurie felt the pain of Marion's humiliation all the way to her toes. She sat immobile, horrified.

Marion's smile faded. "You think I don't . . . look the part. Be that as it may, gentlemen, men do gravitate to me. It may be something mysterious to you, perhaps, but men want me."

"Perhaps in your fantasies," Bottoms said brutally. "This situation is not our error in judgment. We have been misled."

Unable to bear the devastation on Marion's face, Laurie turned away, fighting back tears.

From the doorway boomed a deep, masculine voice. "My God, I'm late."

Eric entered, dressed in navy slacks and a double-breasted, brass-buttoned sport coat over a dark, turtleneck sweater. He might have stepped from a fashion ad on a page of a yachting magazine, so astoundingly handsome that his appearance caused a stunned silence to hover in the subtle scent of his expensive cologne. The sight of him set Laurie's heart pounding.

With a confident swagger he stepped to Marion's chair, bent down and kissed her hand. "My darling, forgive my tardiness."

Turning to the speechless gentlemen who sat stiffly in their chairs, he extended his hand. "Eric Sinclair," he said.

Marion stuttered introductions.

"I trust the negotiations are going splendidly," Eric said. His accent had smoothed. "Mind, I've not read the manuscript myself, because jealousy simply will not permit it. To love Margo is to know one could never hold on to such a woman, but what can a smitten man do? I don't know her secret, gentlemen, perhaps no man ever will, but I can tell you there is something about this woman that drives men like me . . ." He paused and looked at Marion adoringly. "Forgive me for embarrassing you, my love. I didn't mean to be so unforgivably candid."

The two lions of the publishing world exchanged intense glances. "Perhaps there is something of human interest here, after all," Bottoms said to Pennington.

"My thoughts exactly," Pennington answered. He turned. "Miss DuBois, perhaps we do have something to discuss."

"I shan't interfere," Eric said, bowing toward Marion. "But I shall wait for you at our usual rendezvous, my darling, and count the seconds until I can hold you in my arms again."

Marion smiled demurely and forced her gaze away from her "lover." "Gentlemen," she said. "One of the world's most luscious secrets is the indomitable prowess of the Englishman in bed. Englishmen are the *corps d'elite* of lovers. They have no competition whatever from any corner of the globe. With the publication of my memoirs, it won't be a secret much longer."

The two Englishmen exchanged glances again. Bottoms adjusted his scarf and smoothed back his thinning hair. A small smile formed on his lips.

Eric was backing from the room. Laurie noticed he was beginning to lose his composure, for he turned away quickly and picked up his pace. She held her breath, hoping he would get away before he lost it.

Laurie rose and excused herself; they were obviously about to start the business of negotiating contracts. She closed the door behind her, thinking, *By damn, Marion was right about the luscious secret of the Englishman's superpowers as a lover. There was no fraud about that!* Maybe even these two outwardly stuffy businessmen knew there was no fraud about that.

Eric was not in the hallway. He had disappeared, probably gone upstairs to change his clothes.

Trembling, Laurie made her way to the back garden. Her eyes filled with tears as the impact of what Eric had just done took hold. Eric couldn't stand Marion. Yet he had exposed himself to ridicule to save her from humiliation.

Laurie's tears flowed with the excess of emotion she could no longer hold back. What had just happened in

there? Was this the same man who had so callously set
her up as a subject in a commercial experiment? The
unfeeling monster who had used her so cruelly? Seduced her when he had rendered her hopelessly vulnerable with subliminal suggestion?

Who was he?

The man she had just seen kissing the trembling hand
of Marion was real and deep and caring. She had believed she'd never know him. But she knew him now.

At least she knew the core of him. Eric Sinclair was
two very different people.

Jeanne Gunn came up behind her. They stood in the
shade of the garden trees.

"I saw what Eric did," Jeanne said. "I saw it from the
doorway. By the saints, I don't believe what I saw." She
handed Laurie a handkerchief from her apron pocket.
"Dropped a tear or two myself, I did."

Wiping at her cheeks, Laurie tried to smile. "Who
was that masked man?"

"What?"

"Never mind. It's just a stupid joke."

Jeanne asked, "Where is he now?"

"Disappeared. Ashamed to show his face, I guess.
Can you imagine him confronting Marion again after
this?"

The two women's eyes met and held. Simultaneously they began to sputter, and their sputters
evolved into peals of laughter.

Jeanne sat down on a bench when her laughter sub-
sided. "I have to say, Laurie, it was an act of pure com-
passion we witnessed, and after the way Marion
constantly needled the laddie, too."

"The publishers bought it, didn't they?"

"Aye. Perhaps because the performance was spontaneous. He was good. The lad can act."

Don't I know it, Laurie thought. She said, "Marion was good, too, the way she took it to the finish with that remark about Englishmen."

Jeanne laughed again. "She could get herself run out of Scotland for that."

Laurie sat down beside the older woman. She wondered if Jeanne suspected something was going on between Eric and herself but nothing had been said and she knew nothing would be. "Jeanne," she said softly, "what made him do it?"

Mrs. Gunn smiled at her. "You know why as well as I do, Laurie. The laddie's good at mischief, true enough, but he has a heart that's full o' human kindness."

THEY SAW NO MORE of Eric that day. Laurie figured he was probably at the Red Wolf, drowning himself in Scotch whisky. Subdued by his performance of the morning, she drove to the standing stones. She was anxious to get away now, both from Lees and from the man with the heart full of human kindness, the man who had hurt her more deeply than she had ever been hurt in her life.

Driving, she recalled last night—his telling her he was dangerous and then holding her so protectively. His behavior was baffling. He was nothing if not a living contradiction. The only thing Laurie knew for certain about Eric Sinclair was that he was trouble. He'd go on hurting her if she gave him the chance. She would not give him that chance.

When she caught herself humming their music, it infuriated her. Would she have fallen in love with him without it? Of course she would have. Laurie knew herself well. The silly tapes didn't really work.

But, thank heaven, Eric didn't know she ever truly loved him. That would be the greatest humiliation of all.

Who was he? The question haunted her. It was always weak men who were cruel; gentleness came only from the strong. She believed this. And Eric? Eric was strong. If he had a weakness, she had yet to see it, and yet he had been very cruel to her.

Cruelty could be gentle, too.

IN THE HEART of the meadow, near the foot of a great old oak, Laurie searched the stones of mystery. Farther down in the swale, nearly hidden by bracken, was evidence of what might have been a place of sacrificial fires. Fires from the festival to signal the coming of winter, season of death, when fairies were free to wander the world and wreak their evil on humankind.

Eric's fairies. Were there superstitions carried in the blood of his ancestors? He himself had said the old beliefs were not dead. But who were his ancestors? What he'd told her about his life might not be true at all. Knowing what a good actor he was, she figured the preposterous childhood and questionable identity were probably lies. She wondered if, whether true or untrue, he had ever told the stories to anyone but her. Could it all have been just part of the "data" he'd been feeding her?

Laurie regretted now that the tattoo would take two weeks to scrub off completely. Two weeks more of looking at Eric's name in a heart on her arm were going to drive her crazy. Her mother had always warned that revenge had a way of slapping back. It had been worth it, though.

Hadn't it?

THE HOUSE FELT DIFFERENT when she returned around seven that evening. Pennington and Bottoms had taken their leave hours ago. Eric's car was missing. Marion was bustling about in the hideous red crepe, talking incessantly. Every sentence began with "Eric" or "My Eric."

No wonder he was gone.

Margo DuBois's contract was still under negotiation, it seemed. But at what price to the rest of them? Jeanne looked haggard as Marion flitted around her like a bird who refused to alight.

Eric was in for it now. Marion was capable of doing as good a job on him as Laurie had done. He must have sent some word as to his whereabouts, because there were only three plates set on the table for dinner. From the knowing glance Jeanne slipped her, Laurie knew Jeanne wanted the chance to talk to her in the kitchen.

They had to wait fifteen minutes before Marion, now cast in the role of Eric's lover, floated out of the room and up the stairway, muttering something about the weather in London.

"I am going to lose what little is left of my mind!" Jeanne Gunn wailed as soon as she and Laurie had ducked into the kitchen.

"But why is she acting like this? She has to know why he did it. She couldn't possibly believe Eric's stupid act!"

"I no longer care. I just want that madwoman out of here." Jeanne turned to Laurie with concern.

Sensing they had not come in here to talk about Marion, Laurie felt a pang of fear. "Where is he?"

"He's left."

"Left Dawning?"

"Left the island. I don't want to discuss anything in front of her, because I won't subject myself to the drama. But he got a call from London. I took the call myself. Afterwards he said he had to go because his father was dying. An emergency, he said." She reached into her apron pocket. "He asked me to give you this."

She handed Laurie a folded scrap of paper, on which he had scribbled. "I'm coming back. Don't leave. Phone me at this number in London. Eric." Below his name was a London telephone number.

For a long time she stared at the note. "His father is dying? That's what he told you?"

"Aye."

"Did he seem . . . upset . . . worried?"

"It was impossible to tell, Laurie."

His father? The one who used and abused him? The one who she assumed had disappeared from his life a long time ago?

"Pennington and Bottoms were still here when that call came," Jeanne volunteered. "Eric drove round to the side and loaded up his car and was gone in minutes without being seen. Afterwards, when I told Marion he had left, she was devastated. She claims he left because he feared she would reject him. She wants to find him in London."

"Great. Maybe he left to get away from her."

"I don't know, Laurie. But he did get the telephone call."

"And he told you it concerned his father."

"Aye."

It wasn't Marion's antics he was fleeing, Laurie thought, but hers. The story about a sick father might be right up there with the story about wind blowing the tape over the cliff. He had no father, according to him.

What did it matter, anyway? Eric was gone.

Jeanne Gunn was studying her carefully.

Laurie said, "This note says he might be back. Did he tell you he'd be back?"

"Aye, but without much conviction. I myself am doubting it. He took everything with him." Jeanne proceeded with dinner preparations, washing vegetables. "I can't see him subjecting himself to the likes of her ladyship now, can you?"

No. Nor to me, Laurie thought, feeling suddenly emptier than she had ever felt in her life.

The only link she had to Eric Sinclair was a scribbled telephone number. Once she left Lees, he had no way of finding her. During their tempestuous times together she had revealed so little of her life. Their romance had existed as independently of the outside world as this little island did. She wrestled with this fact during the night. It would have been easier for Laurie if the Marion incident had never happened. If she'd never known he had a heart.

Was it possible he really did have a father who was dying? If his father was dying, Eric was having a difficult time right now. And if the father story was untrue, why would he lie about it?

Laurie knew she couldn't leave without some answers. Wondering for the rest of her life would drive her mad.

The next morning she dialed the London phone number. She wasn't fooling herself entirely. The idea of never hearing his voice again was too hard to take. He'd realize this, of course, but he wouldn't blame her; he'd blame the tape. Her fingers trembled as she dialed.

"Aquarius Recordings," a male voice answered. It was not Eric's voice. His business number, she thought. Not his home.

"May I speak with Eric Sinclair, please?"

"He isn't in. If you'd like to leave a message, he'll return your call."

"No. I'm just calling to inquire about…" She paused. "Someone told me you sell subliminal love tapes."

"I'm sorry," the man said in an accent more clipped than Eric's. "The love tapes have been discontinued. They're off the market."

Something pulled inside Laurie, a pain she couldn't identify, at least not yet. "The tapes aren't available?"

"Not since yesterday. Sorry."

"Can you tell me why?"

"Our product analyst pulled them out of production."

"Would your analyst be Eric Sinclair?"

"It would. Look, I can send you a catalog. We have a good selection of subliminal message tapes on other subjects."

"No . . . thank you."

By the time she set down the receiver, Laurie was trembling. Eric had pulled the tapes out of production. Her reward had paid off superbly. She was the victor. She ought to feel terrific.

But she didn't.

Why had he done it? He believed the tapes worked— really worked. Laurie felt light-headed as she sat down on the bottom step of the stairway and tried to think. What other explanation could there be for discontinuing production of the tapes, unless he didn't want what he thought had happened to her to happen to somebody else? Could this have had anything to do with his return to London yesterday? What had that call really been about? But if it was business that took him home, why wasn't he in his office?

I don't care where he is, she scolded herself. *I mustn't care!*

Marion was in the breakfast room singing. Laurie walked past her with barely a smile and into the kitchen, where her hostess was finishing the morning dishes.

"Jeanne, I've got a stain in the car I don't want to get charged for," she lied. "I need the strongest cleaning detergent you have."

"This ought to take it out," Mrs. Gunn said, reaching for a bottle on the shelf.

"Thanks."

Laurie took the wide steps two at a time, closed herself in the upstairs bathroom and took off her sweater and blouse. The detergent stung her skin, but she kept scrubbing until her arm ached. With gritted teeth, she determined to scrape off the first two layers of skin, if that was what it took to get off that cursed heart with Eric's name in it.

When she could stand no more of the pain of scrubbing, the tattoo was barely visible. Like Eric himself—almost gone.

LAURIE COULDN'T SLEEP. Washing away his name wasn't going to wash away the man. The thing with Eric was unfinished.

He had pulled the tapes off the market because of her lie. How many people stood to lose substantial amounts of money because of her lie? Just what I needed, she told herself in the stillness of the Highland night. Guilt.

But guilt wasn't the only thing keeping her awake and she knew it. What was unfinished had to do with her victory. *A battle isn't won until the enemy knows he's lost,* she reflected. Eric hadn't even known there was a battle!

One way or another, she was going to have the satisfaction of telling him.

IT TOOK ANOTHER DAY to gather the courage to phone him. Ignoring a premonition of doom, she dialed Aquarius Recordings and once again asked for Eric.

"Eric isn't in," the man told her. "May I take a message?"

She hesitated. "I'm a concerned friend, just calling to inquire about his father."

"His father?"

"I understand his father is quite ill."

"I . . . uh . . . I'm unaware of this. Are you sure you're not mistaken?"

Another lie. It didn't surprise her. Eric's lies couldn't surprise her anymore. She asked, "He does have a father?"

The man's discomfort sounded in his voice. "He hasn't mentioned an illness in the family."

"I see. Could you please tell him—"

"Hang on," he interrupted. "Eric has just walked into the office. One second. . . ."

Not one, but several tense seconds passed before she heard his voice. "Sinclair here."

"Eric, it's Laurie."

"Laurie! I was going to phone you this minute when I got in."

"How is your father?" she asked.

A short silence. "I'd rather not talk about that right now. How much longer will you be on Lees? I must see you."

"Why?"

"What do you mean, 'why'?"

Anger over the lie about his father helped. It reminded her of the other falsehoods he had told her in the passion of the night.

"Eric," she began slowly, trying to savor her moment of victory. "I phoned because there is something I want to tell you before I leave."

12

"I DON'T LIKE the sound of your voice," Eric said. "What is it?"

His tenseness came through the wires. Laurie closed her eyes. She ached to tell him she knew what he had done and that her love was as much a lie as his—just a silly act. But the glow of satisfaction was dampened down by pain.

She hadn't predicted this pain. Her heart was betraying her—telling her that when she hung up this phone, she would never in her life hear his voice again.

"What is it?" he repeated.

"The...uh...music..." she stammered. Desperately she called back her best ally—anger. The anger lurked, red and throbbing, just under the surface of her pain, but the damned pain wrapped itself around her anger and would not let it out. It threatened to seep out in sobs.

Crying would never do! She couldn't let him hear her anguish. But good as he was at reading emotions, he probably knew already that there were tears in her eyes.

"Laurie? What about the music?"

Anger...hurt...humiliation turned to salty liquid, spilling down her cheeks. This was to have been her moment of triumph—and all she could think about was that it was the last time she would ever hear his voice.

"The . . . music . . ." she repeated like a robot.

"Are you still upset because I lost that tape?"

She didn't answer.

"Look, sweet, don't be sad. I'll get you another."

"How kind."

"Something is very wrong," he said. "What is it?"

Her voice came soft and shaking, through teeth gritted in anger—anger at herself as much as at him. Anger because she couldn't tell him. She couldn't stand here and tell him what a fool he was, no matter what he'd done to her.

"Goodbye, Eric," she said softly. "I just wanted to say that . . . that the least, the very least you could have done was to . . . to . : . really have been a Gypsy!"

He could hear her agony, her tears, and she knew it. Muffling a sob, Laurie hung up the phone.

So much for the great victory. Never in her life had she hurt so deeply.

Two minutes later the telephone began to scream, torturing her. Mrs. Gunn and Marion were in the garden. Laurie closed her eyes and let it ring.

When finally the ringing stopped, she gathered up her notebook and camera from the hall table and went outside to her car. The skies were hazy, but the breeze blowing in from the ocean was gentle and uncommonly warm. It was a world within itself, this remote island. All her life she would remember the mysterious, fog-blown Isle of Lees.

She would remember him.

Marion was at the door, huffing and breathless. "Did I hear the telephone? Didn't you answer it? Was it him?"

"Who?"

"Eric, of course. He'll be phoning for me."

Laurie stared her down. "I didn't answer it." *I can't take any more of this*, she thought.

"He'll phone back," Marion said as Laurie started down the winding, stone path toward her car, anxious to get away, out to the Celtic sacrificial site. The drawings and photographs were yet to be done, because in her distracted state of mind she had procrastinated. The notes, however, were nearing completion.

In the afternoon rain clouds moved in, threatening a downpour, forcing her to leave before she was ready.

She came in late for tea.

"I was afraid you weren't watching the sky and you'd get soaked," Jeanne Gunn said.

Laurie helped herself to tea and biscuits. "All I needed was another two hours. Now because of the rain, I'll have to stay another day and catch the ferry Sunday."

"The ferry doesn't cross on Sunday."

"Oh, I'd forgotten that." Escaping the island had become urgent for Laurie, the uncooled memories too painful.

Marion sat stiffly, sipping tea. "He hasn't phoned back. I know you're dying to ask."

Laurie gazed at her in silence.

Jeanne Gunn's lips tightened to a thin line. "My dear Marion. The laddie did you a fine deed of kindness. You'd do well now to let it rest."

"Kindness? A man like Eric Sinclair does not act out of kindness. He is motivated solely by lust."

Laurie exchanged helpless glances with Jeanne Gunn. Surely Marion knew she wasn't fooling either of them?

"So you must leave, Laurie," Jeanne said. "I'll be sorry to see you go."

"I'll miss the peace of Lees," Laurie answered. "I don't want to wait until Monday, though. I think I'll pack tomorrow, drive to the standing stones and finish up my notes there and then drive on around to Fyfe's Landing. If I get an early start, I can make tomorrow's ferry."

"I'll pack you a bit of lunch to save you time." Jeanne turned suddenly and looked up. "Marion, turn down the radio. I thought I heard someone coming."

The door of the parlor opened. A dark form filled the door frame.

"I'm late for tea," he said.

Marion sat forward with a start. "Eric!"

Laurie shrank back into her chair. She'd been afraid he might return. She'd planned to be gone before he did. "How did you get here so fast?"

"Ever hear of planes?"

"A charter?" Marion almost purred. "You were eager to return."

"Yes." He barely glanced at her. His eyes came to rest on Laurie. "We have to talk," he said.

She forced a smile for the sake of the others. "We never really talk, Eric. You never have anything to say."

"I have a great deal to say."

"What have you to say to me?" Marion asked.

He turned. "What?"

"To me? After the morning my publishers were here."

Eric rubbed his chin with impatience. "Are you going to get the book contract?"

"Possibly. Probably. There is still the final decision to be made by the publicity people in London. I shall go for photographs and interviews soon, and I thought perhaps you would go with me. Have photos taken with me."

His eyes narrowed. "You know better, Marion. Damn it, you know better. You and I have never been friends."

Her hard gaze held his until he had to turn away. "Why did you do it, Eric?"

"Hell, how do I know? I wouldn't have if I'd thought you were going to make me pay. Let's drop it, shall we?"

"Do you want tea?" Jeanne asked nervously.

"No, no tea."

Mrs. Gunn rose to her feet, smoothing the front of her dark woolen skirt. "How is your father?"

"He died a few hours after I got to London."

Laurie drew in her breath. His eyes held no emotion at the mention of his father. Deceit was as easy to Eric as breathing.

"I'm sorry," Jeanne said.

"I'm sorry, too," Laurie offered without sincerity.

Marion rose. "My condolences also." Her voice was icy. She looked at her watch as if she had an appointment and went quickly to the door. Eric had called her bluff. He had ended the issue of their last encounter without ceremony or apology.

Mrs. Gunn gathered up the tea tray.

"I want you to tell me exactly what you have on your mind," he said to Laurie.

She waited until Jeanne had left the room before she answered. "We don't have anything to talk about."

"Why did you phone me in London, then?"

"To inquire about your father."

He moved around in front of her. "How about the truth?"

She looked away. Having tricked him by lowering herself to his level didn't feel good anymore. The less said now, the better.

"Something has happened," he said.

She glanced sideways, then back. "Why did you leave?"

"You already know—the summons about my father."

"The father who stole you from the Gypsies. Whose illness your office didn't even know about. Are you grieving for him?"

"Not particularly. I doubt he really was my father. My business partner doesn't know about my personal life. I was called by the nursing home where the old man has been for the past five months. He was dying and asked for me. I half expected a confession from him— a revelation about my past—but no, he stuck with the Gypsy story to the end. He wanted to give me a key to a bank box where he'd stashed over fifty thousand pounds—his gift to me. He gave me the bloody key and then he died smiling."

A catch in his voice as he tried to lighten the heart-wrenching story gave him away. Laurie felt the pain he tried to conceal. *He'd have rather had the father than the money*, she thought. "Was there fifty thousand pounds?"

"There was. And an old photo of the two of us to-gether, and a baptismal certificate. The old boy had me baptized, though he'd never mentioned it and I don't remember. He had no use for religion as far as I ever knew. But I didn't come to talk about my father. You said on the phone you were leaving. Would you do that? Just leave me?"

Her head swam. As far as Eric knew, she was still under the spell of subliminal commands. He hadn't finished the research and needed her. Damn it, why hadn't she just left when she found out, instead of playing that stupid revenge game?

"I'm going home," she said.

"Just like that?"

"Yes."

"What about us?"

"There is no 'us.' I thought I loved you, but it seems to have worn off."

He looked devastated. "Worn off?"

"Strange, isn't it?"

"Then it wasn't me? None of it?"

"What do you mean? What else could it have been?"

"Laurie, how could you change so much in just a few days? Look, I'm sorry I had to leave so abruptly."

She straightened and took a deep breath. This conversation was agony. "Right after your stunning performance with Miss Margo DuBois."

"Good Lord, that can't be what this is about!"

She laughed without humor. "No, of course not. It was a brave and noble deed you did. It touched me. I had no idea a Gypsy such as you . . ."

He touched her shoulder. "Speaking of which! What was that remark you made before you hung up the phone this morning? About how I could at least have really been a Gypsy? Do you think I've lied to you about my life?"

"I . . . actually, yes."

"With what possible motive?"

She forced a smile. "To tantalize."

"A sordid background like mine—one I'm anything but proud of? Tantalize?"

"Yes, and you know it. That's why you have it."

Confusion darkened his face. "Laurie, look. I don't know what's wrong, exactly, but you're pulling away from me and I don't like it. I thought you cared for me."

She prayed he wouldn't notice her trembling. "Do you care about me?"

"You must know I do. We have something together. We have something to build on."

Laurie shook her head. "There's nothing to build on."

"Something's gone bloody wrong, then."

You'd better believe it. Your brainwashing didn't hold. "Did you . . . uh . . . bring the tape?" she asked.

"Yes. And some others I thought you might like."

"What others?"

His voice caught, the way a child's does sometimes in a lie. "Just music I thought you'd enjoy listening to."

Her stomach knotted in a hard ache. "Thanks. It'll be music to remember you by." The anger kicked back, hard, all over again.

He reached into the small suitcase he'd set by the door and handed her a blue plastic sack with Aquarius Recordings printed on the side. In it were two audio cassette tapes.

Laurie gripped the bag, struggling with her fury. He was back into devilry again, trying to use her again . . . to brainwash her into cooperating. "I'll keep these forever."

"Let's go upstairs where we can be alone."

"And listen to these tapes?"

"Sure. While we talk about your staying with me."

"No, Eric. I'm going home."

His eyes turned a strange color of silver. "You feel nothing for me?"

This time she couldn't look at him when she lied. "I thought I did, but not now." Starting to feel sick, she had to get away from him and fast. "There's nothing left to say except good luck to both of us."

"Laurie..." he began. With a sudden intake of breath he stopped himself. There was a deadly, frightening silence. His jaw went tight.

She stepped back in fear. There was a dangerous side to this man, she'd always known it. Now she was witnessing it. Something wild and awful had leaped into his eyes and silenced his voice. His hands were twisted in tight fists. Was it outrage at being rejected? *Please*, she prayed silently. *Just let me go!*

When she started to inch away, he grabbed her arm. "Something's missing here, isn't it?"

Laurie followed his eyes. He was looking at the tiny, remaining ink smudge, where the heart had been with his name in it!

She was too surprised to come back with an answer. The silence in the room felt ice-cold.

He released her arm. "Then it wasn't real!"

"Nothing was real, Eric! Not me. Not you. When I found out you had a game going, I decided to play. It was a stupid decision, I know now. But I was too hurt to think straight."

His voice dropped almost to a whisper. "What are you talking about?"

"I think you're rapidly figuring it out. I know I was wrong, but you started it. Your damn subliminal persuasion tapes started it. How could you do such a thing to me, Eric?"

His eyes changed color strangely. "When did you find out?"

"Not before you managed to seduce me, damn it to hell!"

Eric stepped between Laurie and the door, so she would be unable to make an exit from the room until he allowed it.

"Wait a minute. Let's back up. How did you know about the tape?"

"That night in your room—the last time we made love—I was looking for a paper to write you a note and I found your 'log' and my name, spelled S-u-b-j-e-c-t. It's a wonder you lived through that night, Eric. I could so easily have killed you."

He turned away and muttered an oath under his breath. When he turned back, his eyes had changed again. "So you decided to go after me in a more effective way."

"It was you who told me life was a game."

"You believed I used the tapes as a means of seducing you?"

"Why else would you do something so underhanded? So manipulative? So . . . rotten? You humiliated me and I was furious. I figured if you wanted to brainwash me with that blasted tape, then I'd make you think you'd been a smashing success!"

"Revenge."

"Purely."

"You did a commendable job, Laurie. You had me fooled."

"Good. You had me fooled, too."

"The tattoo was very creative. I had nightmares about you having to have it surgically removed."

She glared at him. "Your name scrubbed off with only a minimum amount of pain."

"Would you ever have told me the truth?"

"I don't know. Would you ever have told *me* the truth?"

His eyes fell. "I doubt it."

She wrung her hands, wanting to run from the room.

"I shouldn't have done it," he said. "But I swear I didn't intend to...." He paced a few steps, then came back. "Laurie, I didn't want to hurt you. I wanted to love you."

"You managed both quite well."

He sighed heavily. His eyes had softened. "For once in my life I can't find words. They're screaming to get out and I can't find them. I can't defend myself. If I tell you how much I care for you, you won't believe me."

"No. As I said, there isn't anything more to talk about. You can put the stupid tapes back on the market. No one else's knuckles will be endangered from the use of them."

He swallowed. "You hate me, don't you?"

"Yes," she lied.

"Then I suppose nothing I can say will change that."

"Nothing."

He moved aside, freeing her passage to the door.

"It might have been pretty wonderful," he said softly.

"Yes," she whispered. "If only you had been . . . authentic." Her hand was on the doorknob. "Good-bye, Eric."

Laurie went to her room and packed. The blue sack of tapes he'd just given her went into the bag first. She'd keep them as a painful reminder, in case she was ever foolish enough to trust a man again. She'd lost her appetite, but because it was her last night at Dawning Cottage, Jeanne would be preparing something special. It would be rude, even cruel, not to go down. Dinner with Eric would be awful, but she could get through it somehow.

Her fears were ungrounded. Eric wasn't at dinner. Jeanne said he had left his bag in his room and then she had seen him leave again. For the Red Wolf, Laurie assumed.

The Red Wolf, where they had first met. Laurie's emotions turned inside out. To be this close to Eric, knowing she'd never see him again, was a new kind of agony. If only she'd never seen the gentle side of him, the compassionate side of him. If only she could do better at hating him for using her. If only she didn't love him . . .

Deep in the night she heard him stirring in his room, perhaps just getting in. She half expected a knock on her door, but none came. Eric was persuaded that she hated him.

When she rose at four, his room was silent. Jeanne had tea and toast ready for her in the kitchen by the time she had her bags in the car. A few minutes later, after a cup of tea together, Laurie said goodbye to Jeanne Gunn.

The early morning was clear of clouds. The air was fresh and cool, but it promised to be warm when the sun rose higher in the sky.

Trying to concentrate on what she had come here for in the first place, Laurie photographed the mysterious stones in the bright, early light. The heat warmed her shoulders as the morning sun moved overhead. It would take forty minutes to reach Fyfe's Landing, driving the northern route around the island, a road she'd never traveled, and the ferry didn't leave until midafternoon. That left time for lunch.

She packed her camera equipment carefully into the car, then walked back into the oak grove that surrounded this mystical place. Two thousand years ago she might have stood here and wondered where these stones came from, who had placed them here. Likely even the Druid priests who'd used them hadn't known. Oak trees would have stood here, connecting earth to heaven, as they did now. Except for the song of a thrush, silence guarded the cold, awful secrets of this place. The meadow grass moved softly in the breeze.

Settling down under the shade of the tallest oak, Laurie opened the box of fresh-baked bread and jam that Jeanne had packed for her. At her back she felt the energy of a great tree that had once been worshiped by those who felt its spirit. Every leaf and seed of it were considered sacred; the birds who nested in its branches were sacred, even the mistletoe that lived on the sap, its blood.

Before her the rolling moorlands of this far island were turning purple with the bloom of summer heather. One lonely sea gull, eyeing her bread with its keen hunter's eye, circled overhead. This magic island...how loath she was to leave it. To leave him . . . the man who would always occupy a space in her heart. She'd given her love willingly to him once and would never be able to retrieve it, however hard she tried. Love was irrational.

No one would ever take Eric's place. It was sad to know that. Her heart would stubbornly cling to him for a long, long time, perhaps even forever. One part of her would cling defiantly to the sweet—and bitter—memories of this island.

In the distance, on the horizon, a horse and rider appeared, bursting the bubble of illusion that only she and the sheep and the ancient nature spirits inhabited these moors. Crofters often rode about on horseback. They had been friendly to her and by now were used to her little hired car, parked by the road near the green meadow of the oak grove.

This rider was galloping at a high speed and seemed to be heading directly toward her car. Laurie sat forward, hugging her knees, and watched as he came into clearer view. The horse was white or gray and very large. It carried a man who rode with graceful ease, crossing the hills at a speed that suggested urgency. Her curiosity began to shade off into a shadow of forewarning. Fear, but not quite fear.

No question about it—he was heading in her direction. She set her lunch aside and stood up. The single figure of man and horse was magnified in the sunlight as they drew nearer—until she could see that the man wore dark pants and boots, a bright red shirt with broad, flapping sleeves and a bandanna tied around the top of his head.

As he rode, a glint of sunlight splashed golden from the side of his head. An earring?

Laurie's heart began to pound wildly. The man who rode over the moors with the speed of an arrow carried on the Highland wind was a Gypsy!

13

ERIC? No, it couldn't be! There were ancient spells in this mystical place and she had fallen under one. The Gypsy riding toward her was only an apparition. He had crossed the narrow road and was sailing over the meadow, nearer... nearer.

Laurie stood paralyzed. How real the apparition appeared! His face come into view.

The Gypsy's face was the rugged, handsome face of Eric Sinclair. A red and black bandanna covered the top of his head; the tails of it were flapping in the wind. A gold loop earring hung on one ear. The red sleeves billowed as he rode the big horse hard, fast, not slowing at all as it jumped a small stream in the meadow.

Her mouth gaped. *Why is my mind doing this to me?* a voice inside her screamed.

Some meters away he began to rein in. He brought the steed to a stop before her, and gazed down at her like a ghost for an uncounted number of frozen seconds.

Then he dismounted. "It's time you believed," he said.

And with that, he swept her up into his arms and onto the back of the horse. Before her breath returned to her, he had swung up into the saddle behind her and kicked the champing horse into motion again.

The voice in Laurie's brain hadn't stopped. *This isn't real!* it howled. But the wind in her face was real enough. Her blowing hair stung her cheeks. The heather passed in purple streaks as they raced across the moorlands. The undulating rhythm of the huge horse beneath her was real. And Eric's arm around her waist was warm and strong and . . . very real.

"What are you doing?" she yelled.

"What any noble Gypsy would do. Kidnapping you."

"You cannot possibly be doing this!"

He laughed at her logic. "This is the only way I could think of to persuade you to listen to me." He urged the horse into a hard run.

"It's mad!"

"Authenticity, you said!" he yelled back against the wind. "If it's a Gypsy you want, it's a Gypsy you've bloody well got!"

She could feel him lean sideways to avoid her hair flapping in his face. So breathless it was hard to speak, Laurie sensed it would do no good to try to find out where he was taking her.

The picture of them flying over the hills—Laurie and her Gypsy kidnapper—took shape in her giddy mind. What if somebody saw this? Laughter began to gurgle up in her throat, but she did not want to laugh. It would ruin the picture completely.

What kind of man would do this? A wild, danger-ous man who would stop at nothing to get his way? A man to whom life really was—as he'd said once—too important to be taken seriously? Hadn't she told him what she wanted? She had told him exactly what she wanted. Hell, she'd asked for this!

A few startled sheep loped reluctantly out of their path. Just ahead, set low in a grove of windblown trees, was a stone cottage. Smoke rose from the peat-covered roof; Laurie could see no chimney. Crofters lived here, but the house must be Eric's destination, because there was nothing else in sight but sheep.

They leaped over a low, stone wall and slowed in the shadows of the trees. To the side of the house was an enormous garden. Three dogs ran out, barking friendly greetings. *I'm dreaming this*, Laurie kept telling herself while she waited for a crofter's wife to appear in the doorway.

But no one came. Eric brought the horse to a stop, slid from the saddle, tethered the horse with three fast strokes of his hand, and without a word, reached up and lifted her down. He carried her with ease up the narrow, stone path, the dogs at his heels. One gentle kick opened the door. The sweet aroma of a smoldering peat fire assailed her senses.

Laurie found herself in a chair in front of a stone hearth with her captor on one knee beside her.

"Do you believe yet?"

She could only stare at him.

He did not smile. "You accused me of not being a Gypsy."

"Did I? Perhaps I was wrong." She looked about the dimly lit room, half of which served as a kitchen with a wood-fed stove, the other half as a sitting room with a table and several chairs. "Did you steal this house?"

"I steal only women. Horses and houses I borrow."

With one fingertip she touched the gold earring. "And this?"

He reached into his pocket and produced a mate. "They come in pairs. Here, you wear the other one."

The circle of gold glinted in her hand. He had bought these in the village, then. Found the clothes, too. He'd been busy since yesterday afternoon. Removing her own earrings, she put on the one he had just given her. "I can't believe you can still get a post through your earlobe after so many years."

"It wasn't easy. But it is authentic, which is the main thing."

The open shirt revealed his muscled, dark-haired chest. His golden earring gleamed in the light from the small window. His windblown hair stuck out in tufts around the bandanna. And his eyes were wild with mischief.

"You *are* authentic! Eric, you really are authentic! An authentic rogue and very possibly a Gypsy!" Laurie sputtered and burst into laughter.

"You're not supposed to laugh, damn it." His words were a command, but his own self-control snagged on her shrieks and giggles and the dam of his resistance crumbled. He sat on the floor by her feet and laughed until he fell back on his elbows, saying, "Stop it, Laurie. This is not meant to be funny."

"No? What is it meant to be?"

"Proof of what I am. Besides, you were leaving me and I had to stop you. Talking wouldn't have done it. But you're my captive now, and either we talk or we will never leave this glen. No one will ever know what became of us."

"You're a man used to having his way."

"Not always." He touched her arm where the tattoo had been. "Was all of it an act, Laurie? All of it?"

"Well, no. Not before that night. That night when I . . . died a little."

"I should have realized something was wrong."

Her voice hardened. "How does it feel to be played for a fool?"

He yanked the bandanna from his head. "By the time I knew that experimenting with the damn tape was a mistake, it was too late to tell you. I was afraid I'd lose you if you found out, which is exactly what happened."

"You thought I was under the influence of it when you . . . when we made love."

"I talked myself into believing you'd have wanted me, anyway." He combed his fingers through his hair. "Laurie, there's a difference between meanness and weakness. What I started was mean. I won't try to call it anything but meanness. But things went rapidly awry and the meanness turned into weakness, for which I'm ashamed as hell. Sleeping with you wasn't part of the plan, I swear. But it was too late. I turned round and found myself in love with you."

Laurie watched his eyes and said nothing; she didn't trust her own response.

He saw the accusation in her eyes and took her hand. "I'm not a man who loves often or easily. But I have the capacity to love completely and hard, Laurie, very hard. My desire for you was beyond endurance and I couldn't fight it. I was the one who was too much under the influence to discipline myself to behave. The spider caught himself in his own web."

Her response was slow in coming. It crept out onto the wings of a long silence. "You caught me, too," she said softly.

He nodded. "But the things I told you—my feelings—none of those were lies."

Her heart's erratic flutters gradually were becoming more welcome as it became clearer to Laurie that her heart was not deceiving her now. Instead it was receiving the breaths of truth between his words, and was responding to the truth with palpitations of pure joy. His deep, velvety voice was saying he loved her. His eyes, pleading for understanding, were saying it. The grasp of his hand said it. But what convinced her past all doubt was the sincerity of his smile.

And the golden earring. It symbolized everything Eric stood for: life is comedy, not tragedy. Life is joy, not sorrow. Life is a game, so why not play it like one? This was how he'd played his desperation. He'd gambled the power of his sense of humor with his trust in hers—along with his faith that she loved him.

More than faith. He knew she loved him.

"The tapes you just gave me," she said. "More subliminal subterfuge?"

"Throw them away."

Her eyes flashed. "They are subliminal tapes?"

He winced. "They're deprogramming attempts—to try to erase the influence of the first tape. Len and I worked all night, night before last, on those damn things. He's going to kill me for this. I feel like a bloody fool."

"Good."

Eric smiled the conquering smile again. He was still holding her hand. The fire sizzled and gurgled, and outside a sea gull cried. The dogs had settled down.

"You're trembling," he said.

"Why would someone who had just been kidnapped by a wild Gypsy and carried off on the back of a stampeding horse . . . be trembling?"

"You're not afraid of me."

"No."

His pale eyes misted. "My sweet, I know I'm a scoundrel and a man without even a name I can claim with honesty. But I'm a man who loves you fiercely."

"And I?" she whispered above the erratic dance of her own heartbeats. "Why did you think my love was real?"

"You showed me in a thousand ways. My trickery wasn't strong enough to compete with your love. Even your revenge . . . hell, it was a reason to be with me. You said it yourself, you could have left."

"Are all tinks as arrogant as you?"

"Arrogance? It's faith you're hearing. Faith that our love is too strong for either of us to walk away."

Their eyes met across the open field of truth and feelings bared . . . met and held, until he swept her into his arms and carried her out of the cottage and down a grassy embankment to the edge of a stream. The dogs had followed only a short distance, then turned back. The bracken-lined bank rose at their backs and great trees shaded them, providing a ceiling of green. He lowered her onto a bed of soft grass and lay beside her under the low-hanging branches.

"We've been dancing on the periphery of madness, my love—driving each other away. Come to me now."

Laurie allowed herself to drift into his love in this hidden shelter, while the whispering stream hummed and gurgled nearby and danced around their secrets.

"It's beautiful here...."

"I wanted to feel the earth beneath us again," he said. "The solid, reassuring earth. The way it was in the cave, the day you proved you loved me. I want our love to bond with earth again, now and forever."

"The earth, our element." She smiled dreamily.

Eric smiled back. "Earth, wind, rain, fire—they all belong to us."

"And the lesser things don't matter...."

"Not if you love me."

"I love you," Laurie whispered.

His lips brushed hers. "Marry me," he said. "The spirits of darkness can have my soul if you ever regret for one single moment that you chose me for a husband."

She reached out to caress his unshaven face. "Never change," she said. "Promise me you'll never become civilized. Promise you'll always be as free as you are this moment."

"Only if you'll be free with me."

"Yes," she breathed.

He caught her hand. "That was a yes! You've consented to be my bride?"

"Yes."

"Even without knowing who I really am?"

"I know who you really are," she said. "I know now."

He kissed her deeply, his body against hers, the soft earth beneath them, and flecks of blue sky above blinking through the umbrella of green.

"Once you promised to love me a thousand ways," she said.

"A thousand hours of making love to you would barely get us started," he answered, moving his lips over her throat. "A thousand days will be only a beginning."

Laurie smiled into his silver-blue eyes. "It's a time for beginnings."

"Great beginnings," Eric whispered back. "Just watch, my love. There'll be a Gypsy moon tonight."

Spoil yourself next month
with these four novels from

— TEMPTATION —

MONTANA MAN by Barbara Delinsky

Picking up a hitchhiker in a blizzard was a dangerous thing to do, but Lily Danziger was already living on the edge. She was running away, destination unknown. Perhaps this rugged stranger would provide the shelter she needed.

DARK SECRETS by Glenda Sanders

When Vanessa Wiggins first reported screams coming from behind her home, Taylor Stephenson dismissed her concerns. He convinced her no one had been murdered; no body had been found. And then the ghost appeared . . .

TO BUY A GROOM by Rita Clay Estrada

Sable LaCroix paid Joe Lombardi to marry her. She desperately needed a complete family to keep her son. It was the perfect business arrangement on paper – unfortunately she hadn't considered her desire to be Joe's wife in *more* than name only.

GLORY DAYS by Marilynne Rudick

Ashby and her husband, Brian, shared a dream – to win the Olympic marathon. Only their passion for each other rivalled their passion for running. Training together, they were an unbeatable team – until Brian was injured. And then Roger Atlee, rumoured to take a very *personal* interest in his women, began to coach Ashby.

Temptations and 2 gifts - yours FREE!

We're inviting you to treat yourself to all that's most daring and provocative in modern love stories, with four FREE Temptations a CUDDLY TEDDY and a special MYSTERY FREE GIFT.

Then, if you choose, go on to enjoy 4 more exciting Temptations, each month delivered direct to your door for just £1.45 each. Send the coupon below at once to: **Reader Service, FREEPOST, PO Box 236, Croydon, Surrey CR9 9EL**

✂ ----- **NO STAMP NEEDED** -----

YES! Please rush me my 4 Free Temptations and 2 Free Gifts! Please also reserve me a Reader Service Subscription. If I decide to subscribe I can look forward to receiving 4 brand new Temptations each month for just £5.80 delivered direct to my door, post and packing free, plus a free monthly Newsletter. If I choose not to subscribe I shall write to you within 10 days - I understand I can keep the free books and gifts whatever I decide. I can cancel or suspend my subscription at any time. I am over 18 years of age.

Name Mr/Mrs/Miss _____ EP8

Address _____

_____

_____ Postcode _____

Signature _____

The right is reserved to refuse an application and change the terms of this offer.
Offer expires May 31st 1991. Readers in Southern Africa write to Independent Book
Services Pty., Post Bag X3010, Randburg 2125, South Africa. Other Overseas and Eire
send for details. You may be mailed with other offers as a result of this application.
If you would prefer not to share in this opportunity please tick box ☐

SPARKLING
NEW TALENT

ery year we receive over 5,000 manuscripts at Mills Boon, and from these a few names stand out as the fresh new talent for exciting romantic fiction.

Never before in paperback, we proudly present:

CHRISTINE GREIG
A Night-time Affair
JESSICA HART
A Sweet Prejudice
JOANNA NEIL
Wild Heart
CATHY WILLIAMS
A Powerful Attraction

t yourself to a feast of love,
na and passion with the
romantic fiction from the
of Mills & Boon's new
ors.

e: £5.80
lished: March 1991

Three women, three loves . . .
Haunted by one dark,
forbidden secret.

ALIX ATKINSON

Boundaries

Margaret – a corner of h
heart would always rema
Karl's, but now she had
reveal the secrets of th
passion which still had t
power to haunt and distur

Miriam – the child of th
forbidden love, hurt by h
mother's little love for h
had been seduced
Israel's magic and the lo
of a special man.

Hannah – blonde a
delicate, was the child
that love and in her bl
eyes, Margaret could aga
see Karl.

It was for the girl's sa
that the truth had to be to
for only by confessing
secrets of the past cou
Margaret give Hannah ho
for the future.

W●RLDWIDE